MW00937210

A Perfect Pony

CHARMING PONIES

A
Perfect
Pony

LOIS SZYMANSKI

HarperFestival®
A Division of HarperCollins Publishers

For my wonderful daughter, Shannon
Szymanski. The patience and love you give
to your headstrong "princess" mare,
Christa, inspires and impresses me daily.

A Perfect Pony

one

Niki Crawford jumped out of the pickup truck almost before it had even stopped. Horses and riders milled about on the edge of the parking lot, and a long, blue horse trailer was backing up to a ramp that led into the stockyard. Floodlights lit the whole area, including the white letters on the side of the building that read LIVESTOCK AUCTION.

"Wait up, Niki!" Dad puffed as he slid out of the driver's seat. "Those horses aren't going anywhere without you."

Niki turned and grinned at her dad, her dark eyes twinkling. He was older than most of her friends' fathers, but the thinning gray hair and the slight limp didn't bother Niki. He was still "good ol' Dad." They had been on their own for as long as Niki could remember. Her mother had died when Niki was young.

Slowing her step, she waited for her father. She felt for the lump of rolled money in her back pocket, running her hand over it to make sure it was still there. A ripple of nervous jitters ran through her. *Tonight's the night*, she thought. *I'm finally going to get my own horse.*

Dad put a hand on Niki's long dark hair, and they walked inside together. "Nervous?" he asked, and she nodded.

"I can't believe it's finally happening," she said out loud.

"You earned it," Dad answered matter-of-factly. "That was the deal. You earn it. You pay for it. You take care of it." He paused. "The hard part's ahead of you."

Niki frowned as she looked into her Dad's blue eyes. "You know I'll take care of it. I've wanted a horse for so long . . ." her voice trailed off; then she added softly, "I can't wait to take care of it."

Inside the auction barn Dad stopped to talk to old friends, and Niki wandered down the aisles. They had come here every Saturday night since Niki was little. Dad came to visit with friends from neighboring farms. Niki came for the horses.

Inside the ring, she heard the auctioneer beginning to sell the tack. She knew they would sell the saddles and bridles, brushes and tools for at least another hour before the horses and ponies were led in.

As Niki came to the first row of horses, she stopped to evaluate each one. She was looking for the perfect pony, the pony of her dreams. Would it be a chestnut or a bay, a pinto or a gray? It didn't matter to Niki what color it was. What mattered was something else. Maybe a certain look in its eye or the way it carried itself. Heck, she wasn't even quite sure what it would be. But she was sure that she would know it when she saw her special horse. She would just know.

In the first square pen was a tall, chestnut thoroughbred with two white stockings. He paced from side to side and threw back his head, his eyes rolling wildly. Sticking her head through the top two rails, Niki peered up at the chestnut. All at once he drew himself up and let out a loud whinny. Niki jumped so quick that she bumped her head on the top rail.

She rubbed her head as she moved on to the next pen. There she looked in at a tiny pinto mare with a young foal at its side. A crowd was already gathering around this pen, and Niki knew that the pair would bring a high price. She called it the "cute factor." Whenever there was a fuzzy or cute or young pony, the crowd would "ooh" and "ahh" and the animals would sell for a high price. She moved on.

Down the row she looked at a sturdy bay pony saddled in Western gear. He looked like a nice pony, but not special. She studied a dapple gray yearling for quite some time. It seemed sensitive enough, but it would be another year until she could ride it. There were two pintos—a tall, rangy looking sorrel and a stocky blood bay. Nothing special. Niki was beginning to get discouraged.

She'd worked so hard this summer, helping on the farm, earning the money the hard way, like Daddy said she had to, and now . . . where was her pony?

Turning back to the blue trailer, Niki watched as the driver and his partner returned from the business office to unload their cargo. The first one off was a magnificent black-and-white pinto with a flowing black tail. Niki felt her heart pound as she watched it come down the aisle, right past her and into a holding pen. But if she was impressed with the pinto, she was totally unprepared for the next one.

Her breath caught in her throat as she watched a pure white mare come off the trailer and down the ramp. The mane hung in long silvery strands and she held her head high. She was calm, Niki noticed. That was a trait she was looking for. But there was even more. A large pony, the mare was just the right height. She picked her hooves up daintily as she stepped through the dirty stockyard, almost as if it was not quite clean enough for her.

"Princess," Niki mumbled. The pony was an absolute princess. Then it came down the aisle right beside her, and Niki felt her heart explode as the mare tossed her head. By the time they had closed the gate of the holding pen, Niki was really excited. She reached back to feel the money in her pocket and she knew it would be enough. "Princess" was the one.

When the men had penned her and the vet had finished drawing blood from her neck for the required health check, Niki sidled closer. The man who had led the mare down the ramp and into the pen was a cowboy with a wide-brimmed hat. Now, as he left the pen, he slapped a sticker on the mare's rump: 56. Princess was number 56. It etched itself into

Niki's brain. The number she needed to bid on would be 56. The cowboy grinned at her. "She's a good one, little miss," he said, and Niki blushed. Was it so obvious that she was taken with the mare?

After the men had left, Niki clucked to the mare and she came right over. The face was long and dish-shaped, like an Arabian, with a tiny teacup nose and wide, deep-set eyes. They were soft and brown and they watched Niki closely as she reached through the rails to pat the horse on the shoulder. Without hesitation, the mare lowered her head and her velvety muzzle settled into Niki's hand. *With a spiraled horn she could be a unicorn from a fairy tale*, Niki thought.

There was a commotion behind her and a high-pitched whine rang out. "I want that one, Mamma! You gotta git me that one over there!"

A heavyset woman with rosy cheeks and a big stain on the front of her too tight T-shirt was coming down the aisle. With her hand clasped firmly in his, she was fairly dragging along a chubby little boy with a crew cut. But the whine had not come from the small child. It had come from nine-year-old Billy Baily. Niki knew him. He was in her class at school and he was a royal pain. Now he was pointing at her Princess.

Then he caught sight of Niki. "Hey! It's N*iiii*ki!" he crooned. "Icky, picky, sticky, Niki! Whatta you doin' here, Icky?"

Niki whirled around with her hands on her hips. "Same thing as you, Billy," she said. "It's a free country."

Instead of answering her Billy stuck his fingers in his ears and twirled them around, his tongue hanging out the side of his mouth and his eyes rolling up.

Niki turned and marched down the aisle, away from Billy and away from Princess. "Some people never grow up . . . Billy!" she said over her shoulder.

As Billy's whiney voice faded behind her, Niki hurried forward. There was a crowd gathered around another holding pen where a pony had just been unloaded. *Probably another "cute factor,"* she thought, but she knew she had to see for herself.

She heard the comment of a lady in front of her before she even saw the pony. "Poor, dear thing," the lady said under her breath.

After pushing her way through the sea of legs and bodies gathered around the rails, Niki knelt down and peered into the pen through the bottom rails. The pony was a little bit shorter than Princess, coal black with four white stockings and a narrow white blaze running down the length of his face. She could see his face clearly because it was hanging down to his knees, which were buckled from the sheer energy of holding himself up. Every rib protruded in agonizing detail and he heaved soft whuffing breaths. If it weren't for the way his spindley legs were braced, he would surely have been on the ground.

Niki's heart, which moments ago had danced with happiness, now dropped to her stomach. She fought a sick feeling that was oozing up from inside of her as she looked into the pony's glazed eyes.

"The doggers will buy this one for sure," she heard someone say and others grunted in agreement.

No! she thought angrily. How could they say that? How could they let the dog food buyers get him before he even had a chance? He had already suffered enough. Then, to die for that . . . to become canned dog food! It just wasn't fair.

Niki's hand snaked through the rails to stroke the pony's long white blaze. Slowly, the pony lifted his black head and met her gaze. He held her stare for a moment before dropping his head back down again. But that moment was all it took.

two

Niki wiggled in her seat and watched as the thoroughbred was led out of the ring, prancing and dancing like a ballerina on his back hooves. She reached into the tub of popcorn that was braced between her knees. Popping a handful into her mouth, she waited for her dad to come back with sodas.

Next, a little girl with two long braids rode in on

the bay pony that wore the Western saddle. Dad settled in the seat beside Niki and handed her a soda. "So, you gonna bid on the white mare?" he asked.

Niki stared ahead at the little girl circling the ring on the pony. Niki had showed her dad the mare, and she thought that was her choice, but she couldn't shake the picture of the broken-down pony from her mind. "Can I buy two if I have enough money?" she asked.

Dad twittled his thumbs and shook his head. "What in tarnation would you do with two ponies?"

"I could take care of two."

"Not until you prove you can take care of one. One pony, Niki. That was the deal."

"But, Dad . . ."

"No buts, missy. How many girls get a pony of their own? Now, it will be your pony and you can bid on any one here, but one is your limit."

Niki watched as the bay pony was led out of the ring. It had gone for two hundred dollars, a good price for a nice little pony. Niki knew the white mare would go for more, but that was okay. She had five hundred fifty dollars. *Think with your head*, she told herself, *not with your heart*. The white one, she decided. I have to have the white one. *What would I do with a broken-down pony, anyway?*

Niki munched her popcorn slowly as the horses came and went from the ring. She listened to the hum of the auctioneer's voice as he shouted numbers and acknowledged bids.

As she sipped her soda, two men led the black pony in. They walked slowly, supporting the shaky body on both sides. With his head down, he looked up at the crowd and sighed loudly. His ribs were heaving with every breath he took, and Niki's heart sank again as she watched him.

The bidding started at a measly ten dollars and went up by fives instead of fifties. A family in the front row put in a pity bid, but a loud counterbid came from heavyset Brandon Bartell, the meat man!

"Twenty dollars!" the man with the family in the front row called out.

"Geez," Niki said with disgust.

"Twenty-seven," Bartell countered calmly.

"He's yours," the man in the front said. "He's not worth it."

"Okay," the auctioneer hummed. "We've got a twenty-seven-dollar bid on the black pony. Going once. Going twice."

Niki stood up and shouted. "Fifty dollars!"

As if in slow motion, the popcorn tumbled from between her legs, spraying down the row of empty seats in front of her, and at the same time every head in the auction barn turned to stare.

There was dead silence for at least thirty seconds. Niki felt herself blush, but she also felt anger mounting. *How dare they treat this pony like—like—well, like dog meat. He's a living, breathing pony, for crying out loud, and he's worth more than twenty-seven dollars!*

The auctioneer had composed himself during those few seconds, and now he continued. "We've got a bid of fifty dollars, Mr. Bartell. Would you like to up that bid?"

"Heck no. He's not worth that. Not even for meat."

Niki steamed inside.

"Going once. Going twice. Sold to the girl in the back there. What's your number, honey?"

Niki rooted in her back pocket and pulled out the cardboard stub with her number written on it. She held it up for him to see.

"Eighty-one," the auctioneer said, and the secretary recorded it in her book. Niki stood up and started to leave, a mix of emotions stirring inside of her. She'd saved the pony from becoming dog food, but at what cost? This was not the pony of her dreams. He wasn't even close.

Before she'd even stepped around her dad, she heard the audience gasp. She turned and saw the princess. The perfect pony was strutting into the ring, her head held proud, her manners impeccable. Niki felt a wrench of anger and pain inside of her and she sank into her seat again.

She watched the perfect pony circle the ring

quietly and a moan formed on her lips. She still had five hundred dollars left of her original five hundred fifty. She turned to her father. "Dad? Can I bid on her, too?"

Dad's eyes filled with compassion, and for a moment she hoped he'd change his mind, but then he shook his head slowly. "You made your choice, honey. I'm sorry, but one is all we can handle."

Niki turned numbly to watch the bidding begin. It went quickly, starting at one hundred dollars. Niki groaned again when she realized that the mare had sold for five hundred fifty dollars, exactly what she had saved. She stood and picked her way out of the seat, heading down to the holding pens. She had to see the black pony. After all, he was hers.

The pony was alone. No crowd gathered around his pen this time. They were all inside, *bidding on the magnificent horses*, Niki thought ruefully. She opened the gate and slipped inside. Her father had stayed in his seat. Maybe he realized that she needed to be alone with her feelings.

The pony was standing in the far corner of the pen. He looked at Niki warily as she entered, but made no attempt to move.

"Hi, little boy," she said softly, stepping nearer as she spoke. The pony raised his head and watched her closely, mistrust in his eyes. "You don't have to worry about a thing anymore," Niki continued. "I'm going to take good care of you."

The pony sighed loudly and lowered his head. Niki slid a hand down his neck, then held his head under the jaw and lifted it gently. The pony looked into her eyes and Niki thought she saw hope. No. It was her imagination. But it did feel good to know that she had single-handedly saved the black pony from certain death. She rubbed his head softly, down the white blaze, running her fingers over the whiskery muzzle.

"Hey, Icky!" Billy's shrill voice rang out. "Bought a real nag, didn't you?"

Niki refused to turn around, refused to look at Billy Baily.

"Too bad you didn't buy a nice horse like me. Look at my perfect horse!"

Niki fought down the anger. She turned slowly, hopelessness settling over her. She knew before she even looked which horse Billy Baily had bought.

The princess looked haughtily down at the chubby boy who held her lead. She picked her way down the aisle and back into her holding pen, her neck arched with dignity.

Billy Baily had bought the princess. *My princess*, Niki thought. *My perfect horse.*

three

Niki could not stand to watch Billy yank the beautiful mare around the stockyard, so she went back inside with her dad to watch the rest of the bidding. Only when Billy was gone did Niki return to the black pony. Then she combed his mane with her fingers and whispered softly to him. "You will get fat and shiny," she promised, "and no one will ever treat you bad again." *It was a good thing she had lots of money left*, Niki reasoned. She would need it for the vet bills, medications, and all the food it would take to fatten up the half-starved pony.

After the last horse had been sold, Dad helped Niki load her pony into the back of the pickup truck. He tied the lead shank to the sideboards and hung a bag of hay in front of the pony. Listlessly, the pony pulled out pieces of hay and munched them slowly.

On the way home, Dad placed his hand on Niki's knee. "You did a good thing," he said. "That pony needed you, and you were there for him. He'll fatten up. You'll see."

Niki fussed with her seatbelt. She wanted to feel good. She really did. But all she could see when she closed her eyes was Billy Baily pulling her princess around the stockyard.

"With all that love you have just bursting inside of you, you'll turn his life around. He'll be a good little pony when you're done with him," Dad reassured her. "He's got a lot of heart to have hung in there for this long."

"You don't think he will die?"

"Heck, no. He's a young thing. He'll come back. You'll see."

"How old do you think he is?"

"I took a peek at his teeth at the auction barn and I don't think he's old at all. I'd say . . . maybe three or four. His molars aren't in yet."

"Three or four?" Niki was shocked. "I thought he was old."

"Mistreatment can make a pony age fast, and that poor thing has had the worst of it. But we're going to change all that, aren't we, Sunshine?"

Niki grinned at her dad. "Three or four," she mused out loud. "Do you think he's been trained to carry a rider yet?"

"I seriously doubt it. He looks like he's been ignored for a long time." Dad put his hand back on the wheel as he turned into their lane. "It makes me fighting mad when I see what folks can do to a pony," he said. "They go out and buy their kids a pony just because it's cute and the kids want it. They don't have time to fool with it, so the pony gets tied in the backyard where it gets outgrown. Then it's neglected until it comes to this." He jerked his thumb back toward the black pony. "He needs to be wormed, washed, have his hooves trimmed, a good grooming . . ." Dad checked off a list of things the pony needed. Then he stopped and looked at Niki. "Anything else?" he asked.

"To be loved," Niki said simply. "He needs to be loved."

On Sunday morning Niki found the pony waiting patiently in the stall where they had left him the night before. He had eaten some of the hay they had left in the rack, and there was a place in the corner of the straw that was smashed down as if he had rested during the night. Niki smiled as she unlatched the door and went in to see her new pony. She carried a bucket with a hoof pick, a curry comb, a show brush, and an assortment of rags into the stall.

"Hi, handsome," she sang out, smiling at her choice of words. With his ribs jutting out and his knees nearly buckled, he was anything but handsome. *At least he seems stronger*, Niki thought. She ran a hand down his neck and was pleased to see that he stood steadily, unwavering on his feet. Just one night of rest, a handful of oats and a flake of hay had made him seem stronger.

She began to rub a rag down his neck and over his withers, gently scrubbing away some of the layers of mud and dirt. "We need a name for you," she told him as she worked. "I could call you Prince," she said, then just as quickly she erased the idea from her mind. He was not a substitute for the princess. "We need a name that is earthy and strong," she mused out loud, "like you."

As she talked, the pony turned his eyes to stare at her, then rubbed his head up and down against her arm, almost in affection. "You're a sweetie, aren't you?" Niki asked him. She pulled the show brush out of the bucket and finished working the dirt out of his neck. He was starting to shine in the spots that she had brushed, and inside she was beginning to shine, too. He was a nice pony, not drop-dead gorgeous, not stunningly elegant, but nice. Real nice.

"Blackie. Blaze. Ashes. Moonbeam." She tried the names on like clothing, tossing them aside just as quickly when she found they didn't fit. "What is your name?" she asked the pony. By now she was using the curry comb on his back, scrubbing in circular motions to remove the dirt and dust. As it rose to the surface, she used the softer show brush to sweep it away.

"Smokey, Cowboy, Berry . . ." She was singing the names out loud now as quickly as she thought of them. At the same time she moved the soft brush down his legs, stopping to pick clumps of mud off with her fingernail before brushing again.

"I like that last one."

Niki nearly jumped out of her skin at Dad's deep voice. "Geez, Dad! You scared me to death! I didn't hear you come up."

"Is my voice that scary?"

"No, I just didn't know you were there."

"Ummm," Dad smiled. "I did like that last name though. Barry. A good name for a boy."

"Daaad," Niki moaned. "I didn't mean that kind of Barry. I meant like strawberry, raspberry . . . blackberry."

All at once Niki stopped grooming and straightened up. "Blackberry!" she said again. "For a black pony . . . I like it!"

The pony turned a narrow white blaze to face Niki. Then he rubbed his head against her arm again and she grinned.

"You like that name too, don't you, boy? Then, Blackberry it is!"

As Dad carried the water bucket outside the stall to refill it for Niki, she hummed softly. Things were going to work out just fine after all!

Dad brought the fresh water in and sat it down in the corner of the stall. Niki put the brushes back in her bucket of grooming tools and pulled out a hoofpick, a metal tool that curved into a point on the end. As she lifted Blackberry's front leg to clean out his hoof, a terrible stench filled the air. Without stopping, she began to pick the v-shaped groove in the bottom of his hoof. But the odor just got worse, until she thought she could pass out from smelling it. Then she noticed that the hoof looked shadowy and it seemed to ooze, runny and gray.

"*Whoa!*" Dad said as the smell reached his nostrils.

Niki dropped the hoof and straightened up. "What's wrong with his hooves? They're soft and runny and . . . uh, disgusting!"

"I saw," Dad said. "It looks like your Blackberry has a bad case of thrush."

Niki felt her happiness begin to slowly seep away. She straightened up and pushed her head into Blackberry's warm neck for comfort. Thrush. It sounded bad. It smelled bad. It looked bad. And it was in the worst place: his hooves.

four

Dr. Booth lifted Blackberry's hoof up until it rested on his bent leg. He checked the outer edge for cracking, then pulled the hoof down so that he could examine the underside. One at a time, he checked each hoof. As he examined the pony, once again the smell rose up, like mist sprayed from a perfume bottle, only it didn't smell anything like perfume.

Niki clasped a hand over her nose and mouth. She felt the tears behind her eyelids burn. Anything that smelled that horrible had to be bad news. *Please, God. Just don't let him be lame*, Niki begged silently. She knew that if a pony could not walk, it could not be saved.

Dr. Booth cleared his throat and put the hoof down. He pushed his wire-frame glasses back up and off his nose as he stood up. "Actually, it isn't that bad," he said.

Niki slid her hands down her face and over her chin and waited to hear more.

"It's thrush, all right. But it could have been a lot worse. You got this pony just in time." Dr. Booth reached into his black case and pulled out a tube. He handed it to Dad, then he turned to Niki. "Is he your pony?" he asked.

Niki nodded and Dr. Booth continued. "Listen carefully," he said, and Niki nodded again. "I'm going to trim his hooves before I go. Then, I want you to clean his hooves every morning and every night. After you clean them, you need to get a piece of cotton like this." He handed Niki a piece of white material. "Wrap the cotton around the hoof pick, soak it with the medicine, and reach deep into the crevices of his hoof. Take care to get lots of medicine into every part of his hoof."

Dr. Booth snapped his black case closed and straightened up.

"Is that all?" Niki asked.

Already Dr. Booth had lifted a front hoof and he was trimming away the deadened edges. He talked as he worked, moving from hoof to hoof with the big pair of clippers. "If you keep his stall clean and dry and use the medicine like I told you, this little guy should be as good as new in about three days."

"Three days!" Niki exclaimed in disbelief. "He will really be better in just three days?" The smell of those hooves made it seem impossible.

Dr. Booth slipped the clippers into his back pocket and gathered up his tools. "Yes," he answered.

Dad carried Dr. Booth's bag to his truck for him. "That poor little guy has a long way to go yet," Dad said, then his voice became proud, "but if anyone can nurse him back to health, it's my Niki."

Dr. Booth smiled and turned to Niki. "There is something else I should have told you," he added. "Exercise him daily. It will make his hooves heal quicker and it will help him gain his strength back, too."

"How did his hooves get that way?" Niki asked.

"Thrush comes from standing around in dirty stalls with manure up to the knees or even from muddy lots. Clean horses and ponies don't get thrush."

Niki grimaced. Already she was beginning to love Blackberry, and it made her angry to think of how horrible he had been treated. *How could anyone do that to my Blackberry?*

Dr. Booth had climbed in his truck and was ready to leave when Niki thought of something else. She ran back down the driveway just as he was about to pull away.

"How soon until you think I can ride him?" she asked.

"I think after a week of good food and nutrition he'll be ready to start." Dr. Booth sized up Niki. "You're a tiny thing," he mused. "You won't hurt him one bit." Then he drove out the lane, the gravel crackling under his tires like popcorn just beginning to pop.

Only a week, Niki thought. Throwing her arms up in the air, she began to spin and dance. The hooves would be better in three days and he would be ready to start riding in just a week. *My pony will get better and be a prince as perfect as the princess*, Niki thought. Then she danced down the lane and back to the barn where Blackberry was waiting.

five

On Monday, Billy Baily started to brag about his perfect horse as soon as he got on the bus. He had been in so much trouble during the year that he had been assigned a permanent seat in the front of the bus where Miss Sherry, the bus driver, could keep an eye on him.

"You should see my horse," Billy said. He turned around to face everyone. "She's tall and white and exceptionally beautiful," he boasted. He slid the word *exceptional* out over his tongue roughly, as if he was trying it out for the first time.

"Whoa," Niki whispered to her friend, Laura. "Billy knows a big word!" Laura grinned.

"Since she is so big and tough, I named her Warrior," Billy continued. "She's a real warrior!"

Geez, Niki thought. Warrior? It was the worst name he could have given to the princess.

Next, Billy rotated in his seat to face Niki. "Hey, Icky," he yelled, so that everyone on the bus could hear. "Tell us about the pony that you bought. Tell us about your bag of bones." Then he stood up. "She bought a real nag!" he yelled.

The girls on the bus giggled and the boys jeered. Niki slid down in her seat. *Billy is such a jerk*, she thought. *He doesn't deserve the princess.*

"Niki's pony can barely walk. He's falling apart at the seams!" Billy burst into a round of giggles at his own joke. Others on the bus joined in.

"Sit down, Billy," Miss Sherry said. Billy

wrinkled his nose at the bus driver's order, but he sat down.

"Ignore him," Laura whispered. "He just wants attention."

"I know." Niki sighed. "But my pony isn't a nag," she said. "He was just mistreated, and he's already getting better."

"Billy should understand that," Laura said.

"What do you mean?"

"Well, I hear that Billy's family isn't exactly nice. My mom said his dad is pretty mean to Billy."

Niki stared at Laura, taking in the shoulder-length brown hair and the soft brown eyes. "I didn't know," she said. *But that would explain a lot*, Niki thought to herself. Such as why Billy was so mean and why he always had to have attention, even if it got him into trouble. She just hoped he wasn't mean to the princess.

By Friday Niki was sick of hearing Billy Baily's picking and bragging. She was glad to have the week over.

After school she dropped her books inside and hurried to the barn to see Blackberry. He was in the small pasture, and he came running when he saw her approach. He let loose with a high-pitched whinny and pranced up to the gate. Already he looked better. The spaces between his ribs were filling in, and he was shiny from the grooming Niki gave him each day. His hooves had healed and they looked normal now.

He's actually pretty, Niki thought, and she beamed with pride! Niki slipped between the fence rails. Blackberry shoved his nose against her with a greeting that was so exuberant that it almost knocked her over. "Easy, boy," she said, but there was laughter in her voice.

She clipped a lead shank to his halter and tied him to the fence. After running a brush over his body to remove any dust or dirt, she leaned into his neck, breathing in the soft warm smell of horse. "Want to give me a ride?" she whispered.

Blackberry turned to look at her, his eyes wide and searching, like he wanted to understand. Niki rubbed his blaze gently. "We'll go slow," she told him. Then, Niki hurried to the barn to gather up the old saddle and bridle her dad had given her to ride with. They weren't fancy or new, but they had been her dad's when he was a boy, so to Niki the tack was special.

Soon Niki was slipping the saddle blanket and then the saddle onto Blackberry's back. She moved slowly so Blackberry could see what she was doing. The pony watched calmly as Niki tightened the cinch. *I bet he's been ridden before*, Niki thought to herself, then laughed when Blackberry nodded his head up and down as if he understood.

A moment later, Niki slipped the bridle onto her pony's head. She led Blackberry to the middle of the field. She leaned over his back and he stood quite still, so Niki slid a foot into the stirrup. In one quick, easy motion, Niki was in the saddle. She grasped the reins and waited for Blackberry to react. But Blackberry continued to stand. Slowly he turned his head around to look at Niki, and his look said, "*What are you doing on my back?*"

Niki burst into laughter—an uncontrolled, unbridled laughter. She had expected him to sidestep, or buck, or take off running. She had expected him to react in some way, but instead he just peered up at her with astonishment. As she laughed, he snorted and shook his head.

Niki squeezed his sides gently with her knees. "Come on boy," she said. "That's your signal to walk."

But Blackberry was staring at the nearby hedgerow, then he stopped and swiveled his head around to look at her again. "*Is that what you want?*" he seemed to be asking.

Niki slid from Blackberry's back and wrapped her arm under his neck, scratching his jaw. "You're something else," she said with a smile.

Suddenly Blackberry's head flew up and he stared at the hedgerow again. Niki stood still, this time hearing a crackling in the undergrowth. It sounded too loud to be a rabbit.

Niki walked closer. She bent down to peer into the bushes and leaves. There, in a gap in the brush, a figure was sitting crosslegged, watching Niki and Blackberry. He was muddy and alone and his face was stained with tears. The figure was Billy Baily.

six

"Billy Baily!" Niki exclaimed, her hands moving to her hips. "Are you spying on me?"

Billy crawled out of the bushes, rubbing the mud from his pants, then running a fist over his face. The effort only caused the mud to smear down his cheeks. "Naw," he said. "I was just watching you."

"It's the same thing," Niki said. "What are you doing here?"

"Where?"

"Here!" Niki pointed down angrily. "Here, on my farm!"

Billy scuffed at the ridges of dried mud in the pasture with an equally muddy work boot. "I was looking for my horse," he said so low that Niki could barely hear him.

"You were what?" Niki asked.

"Looking for my horse!" This time Billy nearly shouted. "She dumped me!" Billy glared at Niki. "Are you satisfied?

Niki felt the smile spread over her face as easy as butter on hot toast. She knew she shouldn't smile, but she couldn't help herself. "That's what you get for naming her Warrior," she snapped. Then she turned on her heel and began to stomp away, pulling Blackberry along beside her.

"Wait!" Billy called. "How did you get that pony to be so good?" he asked.

Niki stopped and turned. Billy didn't seem the same. He wasn't taunting. He wasn't teasing, and he wasn't picking. He wasn't being mean. He was serious.

"Billy." She sighed. "Why should I tell you? All you ever do is pick on me and embarrass me in front of my friends."

Billy looked like he was about to cry, and by the look of his face, Niki felt sure he had already been crying. She felt her mood soften. As much as she didn't want to, she was beginning to feel sorry for Billy. Instead of answering his question, she asked him one. "Why did Prin—I mean, Warrior, dump you?"

Billy shrugged. "I don't know." He reached over to stroke Blackberry. "I wanted her to run so I gave her a whack with the crop and she just bucked me off—as easy as that." He raised his palms up. "Then she ran away."

"You whacked her!" Niki could feel her blood begin to boil. That same old feeling of anger began to burn inside of her again. "You whacked a beautiful horse like that. She's a princess!" Niki exclaimed. "But you—you—" she stuttered with anger. "You are a *toad*."

Billy stared at Niki, wide-eyed but calm, as she exploded. "I am not a toad, Niki. Sometimes I act like one. But I am not a toad."

"Only a toad would whack a horse with a crop. If you aren't a toad, then why did you do a thing like that?"

"My dad told me to. He said that was how to make a horse go."

Niki rubbed Blackberry's neck. She didn't know what to say. If Billy's dad hit horses, would he hit Billy, too? Niki hoped not. Blackberry stretched his nose down and sniffed Billy's boots. Then a long tongue snaked out and he licked the toe of Billy's boot.

"Billy," Niki said. "You don't have to hit a horse to make it go. You asked me how I got Blackberry to go so good. Well, I'm going to tell you. It wasn't by hitting him. It was by loving him. My dad says if I love and respect Blackberry, he will love and respect me, and that will make him *want* to do what I ask."

Billy had moved closer to Niki now and he rubbed his dirty face again. His blond hair stuck up in spikes like an over-grown crewcut.

"You wouldn't respect someone who hit you, would you?" Niki asked.

Billy looked down as if in thought, and he scuffed his toe in the dirt again. Then slowly he shook his head. "No. I don't," he said simply. Niki felt the impact of the words hit her and at that moment she wished she liked Billy Baily, because she didn't want him to hurt anymore.

Impatient with standing so long, Blackberry began to paw the dirt with his front hoof. Niki reached over and unhooked the lead shank so that he could wander away, but he only went a few feet, then turned to watch them with a look of curiosity.

"How did you get him to look so good, so fast?" Billy asked. "No offense, Niki, but he was practically dead the night you bought him. Now, he shines."

"He just looked half dead," Niki answered. "My dad says mistreatment can make a horse age fast. Blackberry wasn't treated very well by whoever owned him before me. But he's treated well now," she added.

"You named him Blackberry," Billy said. "That's a good name. It fits him."

"Thanks," Niki said. She wanted to tell him that Warrior was a terrible name, but she didn't.

"Will you help me find Warrior?"

Niki didn't want to leave Blackberry, but it was starting to get dark and Billy looked like he would cry, so she nodded.

"Thanks, Niki." Billy squeaked. "You have a way with horses. And if I don't find Warrior, my dad will kill me."

Niki's eyes widened.

"Don't look like that, Niki," Billy said. "He won't *really* kill me, but I'll be in big trouble."

"Then let's get moving," Niki said. "Which way did she go?" And with that Niki followed Billy through the hole in the hedge and across the big back pasture.

seven

Billy led the way down an old dirt path, through a field of weeds and scattered briar bushes. Niki followed him silently for a while. As they walked, Niki scolded herself. After all the things Billy Baily had done to her, she couldn't believe she was out helping him find his horse.

"After Warrior dumped me she ran past your house, and then up that hill," Billy said. He pointed to the top of a grassy hill. It wasn't far at all. It was a hill that Niki could see from Blackberry's pasture. There was a small grove of trees at the top.

"Why didn't you go after her?"

Billy's shoulders slumped. "She wouldn't let me come near her. Every time I came close, she just danced away. Then she took off and up the hill. That's when I heard you talking to your pony. I was out of breath, so . . ."

Billy paused and rubbed his face. Niki wondered if that was when he had started to cry.

"So I stopped to rest and watch you," he said.

Billy was gazing right into Niki's eyes and it made her nervous. She looked away, picked up her step and started up the hill. The trees were shadowy, especially in the pre-dusk light, but she thought she saw something moving between the trunks and branches.

Billy was looking into the trees, too. "Do you think that's her?" he asked.

Niki shrugged, then broke into a jog. As she entered the grove of pines and whispering maple trees she felt the silence envelop them. She stood still. Breathing heavily from her run, she swiveled her head to look around, scanning the trees. A crunch of brush disrupted the stillness.

"It's her. There she is," Billy whispered loudly.

As quickly as Niki's eyes found the white princess, the princess had found them, too. Her ears were at attention. She had heard Billy's loud whisper and now intently she watched Niki and Billy.

Billy moved forward. His hand was outstretched and he whispered gentle-sounding words, but the princess was having none of it. She snorted and side-stepped as Billy tried to approach her, then danced away. Her head held high, she stayed just out of Billy's reach.

When he had had enough, Billy dropped his hand to his side and stomped over to Niki. "Do you see what I mean? Ohhhhh!" He swung his fist at a hanging branch. "How will I ever catch her?" he whined.

"Let me try," Niki offered.

She moved toward the mare quickly but quietly,

her palm outstretched, but curled up, as if a treat might just be inside for the mare's taking. At the same time she sang out a string of silly words. "You are such a princess pony. I wish you were my own. If I give you a carrot and promise you a bag, will you follow me back home? Come on, princess, come on a little bit. Or I'll sing silly songs 'til you can't stand it!"

Niki sang her made-up song in calm and quiet tones, keeping the words low and steady. Her dad had once told her that it was the tones that calmed a horse, not the words that were being said. As she sang, Warrior's head came up. Her ears came up, and she stopped prancing, too. She stared at Niki a moment, then lowered her head and ambled over, planting her nose right in Niki's palm.

Niki grasped the bridle firmly, pulling up a trailing rein, and Billy burst into laughter. "You are a nut." he said between the giggles. "A certified fruitcake! Where did you ever hear a song like that? Boy, you ought to sing that one to us on the bus!"

Niki felt her face begin to burn. *Why did I bother to help him?* she asked herself. *He'll never change!* She whirled around, gritting her teeth in anger. "For your information, I made that song up," she said. "You can laugh all you want, but I am the one who caught your horse."

Billy stopped laughing, but Niki wasn't through with him yet. "She wouldn't come to you, and I don't blame her!"

Billy's shoulders had dropped and he looked astonished. "I—I—didn't mean to make you mad," he said. "I was just joking around."

"It wasn't funny." Niki sniffed. "I should just turn her loose again and let *you* catch her!"

A look of fear crossed over Billy's face. "Don't! Don't let her loose," he stammered. "I'll be nice to you, Niki. Just don't let her loose."

Niki tugged on Warrior's bridle, leading the pony through the trees to Billy. "Fine," she said. "Here's your pony. But you better keep your promise, or I might be the next one telling stories on the bus."

"I will," Billy said. He stubbed his toe against a stone nervously. "Uh, thanks, Niki," he said quietly.

"You're welcome, I guess," answered Niki.

"Hey! Do you want to walk Warrior home with me?"

Niki looked up at the graying skyline. "I'll go part way," she said. "Dad will be home from work soon, and he'll be wondering where I am, so I don't want to be gone too long."

As they ambled down the hillside, Billy clutched one side of Warrior's bridle and Niki held the other. The mare's long strides fairly carried them along.

"You really have a way with horses, Niki Crawford," Billy said, and Niki beamed.

eight

"I think I'll ride her the rest of the way." They had reached the bottom of the hill when Billy came to this decision. "Will you hold her for me while I get on?"

"Sure," Niki said. She looked at the princess mare and she felt a tiny bit of resentment rising up inside of her. She had caught the pony, and now *he* would ride her.

Billy pulled Warrior over to a rock in the meadow. While Niki held the bridle firmly, he slid onto the white mare's back. As he gathered the reins up in his hands, Niki let go of the bridle. Billy gave Warrior a kick.

It happened so fast. As soon as Billy kicked the mare she rose up, until for one split second she looked to Niki like the statues she had seen in the battlefields of soldiers on rearing steeds. But unlike the soldiers, Billy Baily went sailing. He landed rump down in a soft, moist patch of grass and dirt.

Instead of running off, the mare stepped purposely toward Niki. She stopped just in front of the girl, head down, and waited for Niki to grab her bridle.

The carnival-like ride he had just taken didn't do a thing for Billy's temper. He came up and off of his rump like a cornered wild animal, all claws and squaw. "I'll kill that mare!" he screamed. "I'll break her of that stinking habit, yet." His fists were curled into angry weapons and he swung them in the air crazily.

As she watched him, Niki felt herself shrinking. This Billy Baily was scary.

He kicked at the bushes, the briars, the weeds. He shouted and stomped and roared. Then, just as quickly, he quieted and a rush of tears came to his eyes.

Niki looked away. Stroking the mare, she pretended she didn't see Billy rubbing the wet streaks from his cheeks. When she next looked up, he was running his fingers through the blond spikes in his hair. "Why does she do that to me?" he asked. "I wish I knew."

Niki was silent a moment. Then she spoke. "Maybe it was because you kicked her," she offered.

Billy's eyes grew wide. "Well, how do you make a horse go if you don't kick it?" he asked.

Niki was surprised that he didn't sound angry anymore. "You just squeeze with your knees," she said. "Real gentle. She will know what that means."

Billy looked from Niki to Warrior, then back again. Niki could see the debate raging inside of him.

"She'll dump me," he said.

"You won't know if you don't try."

Billy looked doubtful, then he brightened. "You ride her," he said.

"Okay." Niki said. She had been hoping that he would ask, so before he could change his mind, she led the mare to the rock, gathered up the reins and slipped onto her back. Niki sat still a moment. Then she swallowed a sudden batch of nerves and squeezed the mare's sides gently.

She needn't have worried. The mare stepped forward with a long, swinging stride, carrying her across the field with ease. She turned the pony in a wide circle, riding her back to where Billy was standing. They walked along a few moments, Niki on the mare's back, Billy quiet beside them.

"Wow." Billy said.

"See?" Niki told him. "All you have to do is remember to be nice to her. No more kicks."

They had reached the back of Niki's farm and Blackberry had heard them coming. He trotted up and down the fence line, whinnying his pleasure to the world. The sun had completely sunk behind the hill and all that was left was a shadowy half-light. Niki slid off of Warrior's back and handed the reins to Billy. "I gotta get in now," she said. "Do you want a boost up to ride Warrior the rest of the way home?"

"No," Billy said. "I'll just walk her. But thanks."

"No problem," Niki said, and she turned to grin at Blackberry. She heard Billy and Warrior moving down the path toward Billy's farm.

Billy had almost disappeared into the darkness when she heard him call out. "Hey, Niki?"

"Yeah?"

"Want to go riding tomorrow?"

Niki hesitated a moment. After all, this was Billy Baily. Then she thought about how different *this* Billy was from the one who had to be the center of attention on the bus and at school, and she thought maybe it would be fun to try. "Okay!" she hollered. "Call me in the morning."

"I will." His voice floated eerily on the shadowy breeze.

Niki slipped through the hedgerow and greeted her pony. In the dusty evening light he looked like a phantom, a gray-black ghost pony, much like the one who had pranced in her dreams for years.

nine

"Does Billy Baily's father hit him?" Niki asked as she shoveled a fork full of eggs into her mouth and watched her dad's face. His brows came together in the middle of his forehead like they always did when he was in thought.

"I don't think so," he finally answered.

Niki stirred the eggs around on her plate, mixing

them with the hash brown potatoes. "Are you sure?"

"I guess I can't be positive. I know he's hard on the boy. But I think it's mostly yelling and intimidation."

"Intimidation?"

"Yes. That's when someone uses fear to get what they want from someone else."

"That makes sense," Niki said. "Billy tried using fear to get his pony to do what he wanted. But it didn't work. Warrior wasn't afraid of him." Niki put her hand over her mouth to cover the smile that erupted when she thought of how easily Billy had sailed through the air. Instead, Warrior had made Billy fearful.

Dad saw her smile and his eyebrows arched into a question, but Niki didn't tell him why she was grinning. "What made you think that his father might hit him?" Dad asked.

"It was something Laura said on the bus . . . and I guess it's because of the way Billy is."

Now it was Dad's turn to play with his eggs. He

looked at the plate as if his thoughts were collecting there, somewhere beneath the mushy yellow-brown eggs and potatoes that he was stirring. "Children learn what they live," he said. "Billy will be what the people around him teach him to be."

"Sometimes he is *so* mean." Niki spit out the words angrily and her dad's head came up in surprise. "I'm sorry, Dad. But you wouldn't even believe how hateful he can be. Then yesterday, he was different. He was almost nice, and I felt bad for him."

"Maybe he wants to be nice, but he isn't sure how," Dad offered, and Niki nodded.

"He asked me to come over to ride with him today."

"Will you go?"

"I told him I would." Niki shoved the last bite of egg in her mouth and chewed slowly. "I just hope he's nice today."

Dad put his hand across hers on the tabletop. "I wouldn't worry none," he said. "You're just what that boy needs. A positive influence. A friend."

As Niki scraped her plate, then rinsed it, she thought about what her dad had said. It sure seemed funny to think of herself as Billy Baily's friend.

Niki rode Blackberry out the front gate and around the fence the long way, until she was on the back trail to Billy's house. She rode through the thigh-high tickling grasses, savoring the feel of the warm day and of her own pony beneath her. Blackberry swayed as he walked, and the rhythmic *swoosh, swoosh* of his steps padding through the tall growth was hypnotic. By the time they reached Billy's house, Niki was so relaxed she just knew that nothing Billy could say or do would upset her.

Billy was waiting inside a round corral with a post and rail fence surrounding it. Some of the posts were leaning and some of the rails looked as if they had been derailed. It was the first time Niki had ever come down the driveway, and she was surprised at how everything looked. From the road the farmhouse had seemed nice, but up close the paint was peeling and the windows were sagging. A winter wood pile had lost its balance on the side of the porch, and an assortment of spilled logs were scattered along its length like sleeping dogs.

Billy was trying to slip a bridle over Warrior's head, but Warrior was fighting him every step of the way. Something about the way the ornery pony threw her head made Niki reach down to pat Blackberry's neck lovingly.

A screen door slammed as Billy's mom came out with a basket of wet laundry to hang on the clothesline. When the door slapped back against its hinges a second time, Warrior sidestepped and Billy looked up. He saw Niki and his arm came up in a wave.

Niki nudged Blackberry and rode into the open area, out of the trees.

"Hey, Niki! What took you so long?"

"Chill out, Billy," Niki teased. "It's a Saturday."

"Warrior's ready to go. How about Blackberry?"

"Blackberry was born ready." Niki smiled at the phrase she had heard her dad say so often. In this case, it was really true. As far as Niki was concerned, there wasn't a more willing pony than Blackberry. Niki slid off of her pony's back and tied him to the gate. He gazed at Warrior, his ears pricked. Then he snorted and let out a friendly nickering greeting, his body trembling. Niki laughed and slid through the rails to help Billy with Warrior.

Billy jerked down hard on Warrior's halter. The mare looked stunned, but she just threw her head higher, away from the force of Billy's weight. "I take it back," Billy confessed. "She isn't ready to go yet, and she may never be at the rate we're going."

"Doesn't like her bridle, huh?"

"No." Billy grabbed the reins and slapped them against the mare's neck angrily. The mare jumped. "She doesn't like the bridle, but she will before I'm through with her."

Niki sighed. It was going to be a long morning if she let Billy have his way. Should she intervene? she wondered. It was only a moment until she had decided. "Want me to try?" she asked.

"Be my guest." Billy snorted, tossing the bridle to Niki.

Niki approached Warrior quietly. Although the horse was tied to the fence and could not run away, Niki still wanted the white mare to trust her enough to slip her head into the bridle on her own. There would be no force.

The same silly song she had sung the day before came into her mind, and she sang it again, softly, rhythmically. The mare's head came down, but Niki did not attempt to bridle it. Instead, she scratched the nose lovingly, rubbed the swirl of hairs in the center of Warrior's forehead, then touched the velvety soft muzzle with a fingertip. Within moments the mare had relaxed. The tension had left her muscles and her eye had lost its wild look. Niki slipped a finger in a corner of the mare's mouth and gently lifted the bit up and over her teeth. Then she pulled the bridle over Warrior's ears as softly as if they were delicate butterfly wings, instead of furry pony ears.

"Wow, Niki. You gotta teach me that song."

Niki handed the reins to Billy and smiled. "It isn't the song, Billy," she said. "It's all in how you treat Warrior. Any creature is going to like you more if you love it and show it that you care. If you are mean to Warrior and she does what you want because she is afraid, instead of because she wants to, you have no trust. I want a horse that I can trust, Billy, so I make sure my horse knows he can trust me."

Billy rolled his eyes. "Geez, Niki. I didn't know I was gonna get a speech."

"I'm sorry," Niki said. "It's just that you aren't having much luck with Warrior, and I think I can help you out."

Billy looked surprised. He leaned against Warrior's side. "Okay, Niki," he said. "Finish your speech."

"My dad says using fear to get what you want is called intimidation." She stumbled over the word, but Billy didn't seem to notice. "It doesn't work. Try love instead."

The even breaths of Warrior and the squeaking

of Blackberry pulling up mouthfuls of grass from around the fencepost where he was tied were the only sounds in the corral. Billy's face paled suddenly and he looked over her shoulder. Then Niki became aware of something else—the feeling that she was being watched. She turned slowly.

Just behind her, leaning against a tree and chewing on a long stem of grass, was Billy Baily's father. Niki realized, with horror, that he had heard her whole speech. He squinted at the glare of sunlight, then grinned, the grass slipping from between his teeth and falling to the ground.

ten

Niki waited for someone to speak.

"Uh, Dad. This is Niki," Billy said, his words short and choppy.

"So I gathered," Mr. Baily said. Pushing himself away from the tree, he moved toward the fence and Niki. "What you just told my boy," he said, "it made a lot of sense."

Niki let out the breath that she had been holding.

Billy's father was an older version of his son, from the sunburned face to the spiky, overgrown, blond crew cut. They even wore the same kind of work boots. "Never realized you could get an animal to do for you like you just did," he said, "but I'm one that says if it works, do it."

Billy half smiled at his dad, his posture beginning to relax as he did. His dad laid a hand on Billy's shoulder. "How about if we try that, son?" he asked. "How about if we try what your friend there said?"

Billy just grinned.

After they had ridden on the farm for about an hour, Niki headed home. Billy had not felt confident enough of Warrior to leave the big farm pasture, but he had treated the pony better and he hadn't been dumped. *Progress*, Niki thought. *At least it's progress.*

As she rode home in the mellow light of late afternoon, the same feeling came over Niki that she had felt on the ride to Billy's house. It was as if everything was right with the world. The birds were singing and flitting from branch to branch in nearby trees. The earth rose to meet her with woodsy, warm odors that were delightful to inhale. Leaves swayed on deliciously warm breezes, rustling like whispering women gossiping on a midday break. Soon, school would be out for summer vacation, and the world would be waiting for Niki and Blackberry to explore it.

Niki patted Blackberry, then leaned down to rest her face in his thick dark mane as they moved down the lane and toward the barn.

Niki unhooked the lead shank reins and rubbed Blackberry down with an old kitchen towel. She rubbed the cottony soft material over his neck and back, then down his legs, one by one. She picked his hooves and brushed his mane and told him stories about how boring life was before he had come to stay.

When she was through, Niki put away her grooming tools and turned her pony loose in the pasture. Leaning against the fence boards, she watched him move to the dustiest corner and lower himself to roll, coating the freshly groomed coat with dust.

He stood again, shaking like a dog just emerging from a pond. He looked at Niki quizzically, then broke into a trot, gliding around the pasture in even strides, picking his white stockinged legs high in the air. He cantered around the field one time, two times, three times. At last he came to a stop in front of Niki. The dust had blown from his coat and he was as shiny as Santa's boot on Christmas eve. The white blaze that raced down his face gave him a comical look and Niki loved it. In fact, she loved everything about him.

You are beautiful, Niki thought, *and I love you*. It came to her that while Blackberry was still a trifle thin, he had grown considerably in just over a week. And in less time than that, she had come to love him. *He* was *the right pony for me*, Niki realized with a jolt. She leaned down to rub his velvety muzzle. "I may not have a princess," she said, "but I sure got a prince. You are my perfect pony."

For more charming ponies
and a collectible pony charm, don't miss:

Turn the page for a sneak peek!

one

Tiffany Clark brushed her long red hair from her face in one short angry gesture. She stared at her older brother Tim, her blue eyes widening in shock at what he had just said.

Thirteen-year-old Tim's grin faded. He dropped the bat he was holding. "I'm sorry," he said. "I shouldn't have said that."

Tiffany let the baseball slip from her hands to the

tall grass of the lawn. "Is it true?" she asked. Her voice was no more than a whisper. "Am I really adopted?"

Tim didn't answer, but as the silence grew wider between them, Tiffany was suddenly sure that the answer was yes. YES. The truth rang loudly in her ears.

"I'm sorry, Tif," Tim whispered. He reached to touch her arm, but she jerked away.

"Then, you're right . . . you don't have to play with me . . . because I'm not really your sister." She mimicked his words even more harshly than he had first said them. Her nine-year-old body shook with the effort of holding back tears. Her hair fell forward again as she leaned down, wanting to hide her face.

"Tif," he said softly, and his voice cracked. This time his hand came down on her shoulder gently. "Please . . . I'm sorry. I was just so mad at you. I don't want to take you with me everywhere I go. Sometimes us guys like to play ball without a kid tagging along."

❀ 2 ❀

She pulled away from his hand, away from the voice and the words that stung like a whip. "Then go play with them," she said. "I'm sure Billy and Mark are waiting at the park. Don't worry. I won't come," she added stiffly.

Tiffany watched him turn to pick up the bat and the ball. He slung the bat over his shoulder and began to walk away. Then he stopped and faced her. "You won't tell Mom that I told you. Will you?" he asked.

Tiffany thought a moment, scuffing her sneaker along the concrete ridge in the sidewalk. Then she shook her head. She wouldn't know what to say to Mom anyway.

As Tiffany watched Tim head down the road toward Memorial Park the hurt settled, crushing down on her like a heavy weight. *She was ADOPTED.* It rang in her ears like a gong. She had never even suspected.

Why had she never noticed before? Tim had sandy-blonde hair and eyes just like Dad's. Mom's hair was light brown. Tiffany realized with a jolt that she was the only red haired one in the entire family. Even her aunts and uncles had fair hair.

Tiffany brushed away the tears that stung her eyes. *At least my eyes are blue*, she thought, *like the rest of the family.*

Tiffany could hear Mom humming to herself just inside the screen door. She was capping a bucket of strawberries to make jam. Soon she would look out the window and see Tiffany. She would know that Tiffany didn't go to the park with Tim.

Tiffany didn't want to face her mother yet. She just wanted to be left alone. She needed to sort out the feelings that were whirling inside so fast they were making her feel sick. Before Mom could see her she ducked through the bushes that divided their yard from the Whiley family's yard. She walked down the driveway and on down the street. She knew where she would go. She would go to the pony farm. She often crept along the honeysuckle lined fence to sneak a look at them.

As Tiffany walked, the early June heat warmed her face. She thought about the argument. Tim hadn't wanted to take her along to play ball with his friends. But Mom had told him to. Now that she thought about it, Tiffany realized that she hadn't even asked to go. Mom was always saying Tiffany needed to get out with other kids, and that Tim should be proud to have a little sister that wanted to be with him.

Tiffany thought of all the times she had wished for a friend of her own. Now, she wished for one even more. At school she sat with Melanie Colmer at lunch, but it wasn't the same as a real friend. It wasn't the kind of friendship that kept other girls on the phone giggling or lasted through the summer. If she had a real friend, Tiffany thought, she could call her now. She could confide her secret. Tiffany had never felt so alone before.

Sighing, she crossed the street and slipped through the hedgerow, walking alongside the vine-covered fence. Tiffany always felt lucky to live on

Chincoteague Island. Other kids dreamed of coming here to see Misty's family and the wild ponies. They came on their vacations. But Tiffany got to live here year round.

She reached the main pony field and pressed her face against the fence board. She clung to the wooden post, watching the ponies that grazed inside the pasture. Everything seemed so different now that she knew she wasn't really a Clark. *Who am I?* she thought, and the tears came.

Through the blur of tears she saw a pony come toward her. It was the same brown and white pinto who always came to the fence to greet her. The pony pushed her warm muzzle against Tiffany's face. Tiffany stood very still. Then, a big wet tongue slopped against her nose and down her jaw line.

It didn't matter to the pinto that Tiffany was adopted. Heck, Tiffany realized, the pony hadn't even known she was a Clark to begin with. Ponies didn't think about things like families and where they truly belonged. *And*, she thought, *they never keep secrets from each other.* Tiffany smiled at the mare, rubbing the dark brown spot right in the middle of the pony's broad white blaze.

Tiffany slipped through the fence rails and into the pasture. She had never done that before. But today was different. Today she needed the pony more than ever. She wrapped her arms around the mare's neck, feeling the warm caress of a muzzle on her shoulder. It tickled its way up her arm and whooshed a feathery breath across her neck. Tiffany inhaled, relaxing a little. The pony smelled so good. It stood still, allowing Tiffany to hold her face against its neck. Tiffany's hurt began to soften and she opened her eyes slowly, rubbing away the leftover tears.

Suddenly, the pony tensed. Her head flew up and she let out a shrill neigh, trembling from her neck, down her shoulders and into her sides.

Tiffany slid behind the mare's neck and peered out, her heart racing. Across the field a tall, thin man with gray hair was hurrying toward them with an angry look. Tiffany recognized Paul Merritt, the farm owner. He was shouting something but Tiffany couldn't understand what he was saying. She scrambled toward the fence, slipping through to the other side.

More trouble, she thought as she slid under the rough barked board. Why had she climbed through the fence? She had known it was wrong, and now, even though she couldn't understand the man's shouted words, Tiffany just knew she was in trouble.

Big trouble.

LOIS SZYMANSKI

is the author of many books for young readers. She lives in Westminster, Maryland, with her husband, two daughters, and three cats. She and her older daughter have four horses—one of them a Chincoteague pony named Sea Feather. When Lois isn't writing, she stays busy taking care of her family, talking to students in the classroom, and dreaming up new stories about horses.

YOU CAN VISIT LOIS ONLINE AT
www.angelfire.com/md/childauth/

❀
A Pony Promise

CHARMING PONIES

A
Pony
Promise

LOIS SZYMANSKI

HarperFestival®
A Division of HarperCollinsPublishers

How and where the seed is sown, as
well as how it is nurtured, determines its final
outcome. So this book is dedicated to my
parents, Donald and Elsie Knight, for all of
their support over the years. The seed became
a tree, with branches you can lean on.

❀

A Pony Promise

one

Tiffany Clark brushed her long red hair from her face in one short angry gesture. She stared at her older brother Tim, her blue eyes widening in shock at what he had just said.

Thirteen-year-old Tim's grin faded. He dropped the bat he was holding. "I'm sorry," he said. "I shouldn't have said that."

Tiffany let the baseball slip from her hands to the

tall grass of the lawn. "Is it true?" she asked. Her voice was no more than a whisper. "Am I really adopted?"

Tim didn't answer, but as the silence grew wider between them, Tiffany was suddenly sure that the answer was yes. *YES*. The truth rang loudly in her ears.

"I'm sorry, Tif," Tim whispered. He reached to touch her arm, but she jerked away.

"Then, you're right . . . you don't have to play with me . . . because I'm not really your sister." She mimicked his words even more harshly than he had first said them. Her nine-year-old body shook with the effort of holding back tears. Her hair fell forward again as she leaned down, wanting to hide her face.

"Tif," he said softly, and his voice cracked. This time his hand came down on her shoulder gently. "Please . . . I'm sorry. I was just so mad at you. I don't want to take you with me everywhere I go. Sometimes us guys like to play ball without a kid tagging along."

❀ *2* ❀

She pulled away from his hand, away from the voice and the words that stung like a whip. "Then go play with them," she said. "I'm sure Billy and Mark are waiting at the park. Don't worry. I won't come," she added stiffly.

Tiffany watched him turn to pick up the bat and the ball. He slung the bat over his shoulder and began to walk away. Then he stopped and faced her. "You won't tell Mom that I told you. Will you?" he asked.

Tiffany thought a moment, scuffing her sneaker along the concrete ridge in the sidewalk. Then she shook her head. She wouldn't know what to say to Mom anyway.

As Tiffany watched Tim head down the road toward Memorial Park the hurt settled, crushing down on her like a heavy weight. *She was ADOPTED.* It rang in her ears like a gong. She had never even suspected.

Why had she never noticed before? Tim had sandy-blonde hair and eyes just like Dad's. Mom's hair was light brown. Tiffany realized with a jolt that she was the only red haired one in the entire family. Even her aunts and uncles had fair hair.

Tiffany brushed away the tears that stung her eyes. *At least my eyes are blue*, she thought, *like the rest of the family*.

Tiffany could hear Mom humming to herself just inside the screen door. She was capping a bucket of strawberries to make jam. Soon she would look out the window and see Tiffany. She would know that Tiffany didn't go to the park with Tim.

Tiffany didn't want to face her mother yet. She just wanted to be left alone. She needed to sort out the feelings that were whirling inside so fast they were making her feel sick. Before Mom could see her she ducked through the bushes that divided their yard from the Whiley family's yard. She walked down the driveway and on down the street. She knew where she would go. She would go to the pony farm. She often crept along the honeysuckle lined fence to sneak a look at them.

As Tiffany walked, the early June heat warmed her face. She thought about the argument. Tim hadn't wanted to take her along to play ball with his friends. But Mom had told him to. Now that she thought about it, Tiffany realized that she hadn't even asked to go. Mom was always saying Tiffany needed to get out with other kids, and that Tim should be proud to have a little sister that wanted to be with him.

Tiffany thought of all the times she had wished for a friend of her own. Now, she wished for one even more. At school she sat with Melanie Colmer at lunch, but it wasn't the same as a real friend. It wasn't the kind of friendship that kept other girls on the phone giggling or lasted through the summer. If she had a real friend, Tiffany thought, she could call her now. She could confide her secret. Tiffany had never felt so alone before.

Sighing, she crossed the street and slipped through the hedgerow, walking alongside the vine-covered fence. Tiffany always felt lucky to live on

Chincoteague Island. Other kids dreamed of coming here to see Misty's family and the wild ponies. They came on their vacations. But Tiffany got to live here year round.

She reached the main pony field and pressed her face against the fence board. She clung to the wooden post, watching the ponies that grazed inside the pasture. Everything seemed so different now that she knew she wasn't really a Clark. *Who am I?* she thought, and the tears came.

Through the blur of tears she saw a pony come toward her. It was the same brown and white pinto who always came to the fence to greet her. The pony pushed her warm muzzle against Tiffany's face. Tiffany stood very still. Then, a big wet tongue slopped against her nose and down her jaw line.

It didn't matter to the pinto that Tiffany was adopted. Heck, Tiffany realized, the pony hadn't even known she was a Clark to begin with. Ponies didn't think about things like families and where they truly belonged. *And*, she thought, *they never keep secrets from each other.* Tiffany smiled at the mare, rubbing the dark brown spot right in the middle of the pony's broad white blaze.

Tiffany slipped through the fence rails and into the pasture. She had never done that before. But today was different. Today she needed the pony more than ever. She wrapped her arms around the mare's neck, feeling the warm caress of a muzzle on her shoulder. It tickled its way up her arm and whooshed a feathery breath across her neck. Tiffany inhaled, relaxing a little. The pony smelled so good. It stood still, allowing Tiffany to hold her face against its neck. Tiffany's hurt began to soften and she opened her eyes slowly, rubbing away the leftover tears.

Suddenly, the pony tensed. Her head flew up and she let out a shrill neigh, trembling from her neck, down her shoulders and into her sides.

Tiffany slid behind the mare's neck and peered out, her heart racing. Across the field a tall, thin man with gray hair was hurrying toward them with an angry look. Tiffany recognized Paul Merritt, the farm owner. He was shouting something but Tiffany couldn't understand what he was saying. She scrambled toward the fence, slipping through to the other side.

More trouble, she thought as she slid under the rough barked board. Why had she climbed through the fence? She had known it was wrong, and now, even though she couldn't understand the man's shouted words, Tiffany just knew she was in trouble.

Big trouble.

two

Tiffany watched the man sprint toward her. His thick gray hair stood up in peaks formed by the breeze and he looked mad. "Young lady!" he called. "You stay right there!"

The last thing Tiffany wanted to do was to cry again, but she could feel the tears forming and nothing she could tell herself would stop them.

He slowed to a walk as he approached her, puffing

a little with the effort of rushing across the grassy pasture. "You are not allowed in the pony field," he ordered harshly. "This is a private farm."

Tiffany leaned against the fence post even though the man was just inches away on the other side. She had lowered her head again, hiding behind her long, rust colored hair. Now she raised her chin enough that the hair slid back from her face, and nodded.

"Young lady . . ." he started again. Then his eyes swept over her and he paused. "Are you crying?"

Tiffany nodded again. There was no use in denying it.

"Well, there is certainly no reason to cry," he said, his voice softening. "I hate to see a young lady cry." He was silent a moment before he went on. "I didn't mean to yell at you . . . but a pony can hurt you if you aren't careful."

The pinto mare shoved her nose between them, rubbing her head on the fence post, acting as if she too were a part of the conversation.

That's twice today that someone has said they were

sorry to me, Tiffany thought. She reached up to rub the mare's forehead. "She won't hurt me!" she said in a voice made strong by her feeling for the mare. "I've come to see her lots of times and she knows me."

He leaned an elbow on the fence post. "I've seen you here before," he said. "You've taken a liking to my ponies, haven't you?"

She nodded again. "Especially her," she said, rubbing the mare's nose gently.

"That's Windy," he said.

What a perfect name, Tiffany thought as she watched the breeze ruffle the mare's mane. "Windy," she said out loud, and the mare pushed her nose into Tiffany's palm.

The man was studying her. Then, recognition seemed to flicker in his eyes. "Aren't you Susan Clark's little girl?"

"Yes," Tiffany said, but inside she heard her mind saying . . . *no* . . . *I don't know anymore*. Windy nosed Tiffany's clenched fist, rooting for attention.

"It looks as though she does know you," the man said of the pinto. "Your mother always had a way with the ponies too."

Tiffany's head came up quickly. She didn't even know her mom liked ponies.

At her look of surprise the man went on. "Your mom used to come here, like you. She was just about your size then, too." He ran a hand through his spiky hair, thoughtfully. "Well, well," he said. "Susan Clark's daughter. It's been a long time . . ." Then, "I guess any friend of Windy's is a friend of mine." Stretching his hand between the fence rails he added, "I'm Paul Merritt, but you can call me Mr. Paul. All the kids do."

"I'm Tiffany." She grasped the hand in a firm shake.

"Old Windy here is going to have a foal in a few months," Mr. Paul said.

"Wow!" Tiffany breathed deeply, rubbing Windy's nose with a whole new look of admiration. Her eyes fell to the bulging left side of the mare and she stifled a smile. And she thought the mare was just fat!

Tiffany grinned. A baby pony!

"See that pinto that looks like Windy?" Mr. Paul was pointing across the field. There was a chestnut yearling and two dark bay ponies. There were some short, fat Shetland ponies, too. And in the middle of them all was a pinto that looked like Windy. Tiffany nodded.

"That's Stormy," he said. "She is going to have a foal soon, too."

"The famous Stormy?" Tiffany asked. "Misty's foal?"

"The very same one," Mr. Paul said proudly. "Windy is her daughter. Now, they'll both be foaling soon."

"Can I come back to see the foals, too," she asked. "I mean . . . I would stay outside of the fence," she added shyly.

Mr. Paul's brow furrowed as he looked out across the meadow. "Your mom used to come and help me with the ponies when she was about your age."

Tiffany continued to stroke Windy as she waited to hear what else Mr. Paul would say.

"I could use a little help around here. Now you're a might young, but there are some things that you could help me with. The stalls always need mucking and the ponies, well," he swept an arm out at the field full of shaggy critters. "You can see they could use a little extra grooming. Would you like that?"

Tiffany grinned. "Sure," she said. "I mean, yes sir. I can do that. I'd love that!"

"Okay," he said. "I'll count on seeing you back here again."

Tiffany's grin spread wide. Nodding furiously, she said, "I'll be back."

"Well now, let's shake on the deal," he said, and he gripped her hand again. Mr. Paul nodded as if he was satisfied and turned. "I got a lot of work to tend to now. Next time you come to call on the ponies you come right in that front gate."

"I'll have to check with my mom . . . but I know it will be okay," Tiffany added.

"I'll be looking for you," Mr. Paul said, then he headed across the field. A chestnut yearling and another dark pinto tagged along behind him as he headed for the barn, but Windy stayed with Tiffany.

Tiffany leaned her head into Windy's neck. She felt the pony's mane fall across her own face and she grinned again, feeling good all over. Then the memory of her brother's news came rushing back and the mix of emotions overwhelmed her.

"I'll be back tomorrow," she told Windy. Pulling up two large handfuls of squeaking grass, she fed them to the mare, then rubbed her shaggy neck again to say goodbye.

She slipped though the honeysuckle hedges and back onto the road. The day had become intensely hot, and as she walked her sneakers popped the bubbles of tar rising in the road. *What will I say to Mom?* she wondered. *What will Tim say to me? Was Mom ever going to tell me the truth?*

Then her questions veered off in another direction. *Who was her mother? Why did she give her up? What's wrong with me*? Tiffany asked herself. The questions whirled in her head, softened by the thought of visiting Windy, pressing her face against the warm neck, touching her velvety muzzle, and breathing the sweet hay scented breath.

Tiffany sighed. Nine was just too old to find out that you're adopted. They should have told her long ago, she thought . . . unless there is a reason they kept it a secret.

Tiffany squashed a big tar bubble in the road as she walked. There had to be a reason, a real reason why they never told her. Tiffany needed to find out. But how could she find out, when she had promised Tim not to breathe a word?

three

Through the window of the back door Tiffany could see her mom still working in the kitchen, so she went in the front door quietly. She plopped herself down on the carpet in front of the television and clicked it on to drown out the hum of questions in her head.

"Is that you, Tim?" Mom called down the hallway.

"No, Mom. It's me," Tiffany answered. "Tim is still at the park."

"Okay." Mom stuck her head into the hall and peered into the living room. Her eyes filled with concern. "Is everything okay? Why are you home without Tim?"

A hard, cold lump formed in her throat and Tiffany swallowed. "I'm fine. I just want to watch television and cool off. It's hot out there."

"All right," Mom said. "I gotta get this jam in the jars while it's hot. Then you can tell me how it was at the park."

Tiffany flattened herself out on the carpet, belly down. She wanted her mom to tell her the truth about everything. She wished she would do it now. Her mom could hold her close and tell her everything would be all right . . . that she wasn't really adopted. But Tiffany knew she couldn't say a word to let her mom know that she knew. She had promised Tim.

Tiffany felt the tears spring to her eyes again.

Sounds from the television brought Tiffany's

thoughts back to the living room. She tried to concentrate on the "Loony Tunes" adventures on the screen. Through the door she could hear her mom humming a favorite hymn from church. Tiffany pushed the mute button on the remote control.

As strains of "Amazing Grace" filled her ears, Tiffany sat up and leaned into the hallway to watch her mother wipe the rims of the jars she had just filled with strawberry jam. Every now and then she smiled as she worked.

Everything she does, she does for us, Tiffany thought, and it surprised her.

Pushing the mute button to return sound to the television, she scooted back into the living room. Just watching her mom had made her feel better.

She tried to remember back as far as she could. A picture of herself at two years of age and still in a diaper came to mind. She remembered how Mom had come to scoop her up from her crib and wipe away the tears. It was a foggy memory, one she wasn't sure was even real. But she really did remember Mom holding her on the back of a large pony at the carnival when she was almost four. Dad had been trying to get her to look at him so he could snap a picture, but she had been too full of the good smell of the pony and the feel of a coarse mane in her hand to pay attention to the camera.

Tiffany went to the bookcase and pulled a photo album from the shelves. In it she found the pictures. The pony she had remembered as big was just a tiny brown ball of fuzz with four hooved legs. He had been large only when compared to her. In the picture Mom held Tiffany's waist and Tiffany held the pony's mane. She remembered she hadn't really been afraid. Mom had made her feel safe.

Turning the pages slowly, Tiffany discovered sheet after sheet of photos. There were pictures she hadn't seen in a long time. Some were of Dad on the boat, or Tim batting a ball. Some were of the whole family. Others were of Tiffany as a tiny baby, then taking her first steps, spinning like a ballerina at one of the dance recitals she had been in, or holding hands with Tim on the beach. The pictures Tiffany concentrated on the most were the ones of her with her mom and dad. She saw the look in their eyes in every picture and it was one of love. She knew a look like that could not be faked, yet somehow it still made her ache inside to look at them.

The back door slammed.

"Hey, Mom! Strawberry jelly? Ummm. Can I have some on toast while it's still warm?"

"Slow down there," Mom said. "Why did you let Tif come home alone?" she questioned. Then, before Tim could answer, "Did you two quarrel again?"

Tiffany couldn't see the kitchen, but she heard the silence. She imagined Tim looking down, wondered what he would say.

"Timothy Clark! I can tell without even hearing it that you had a fight. Can't you get along with your little sister? What was it about this time?"

The tiny knot Tiffany had carried in her stomach all morning suddenly expanded until it felt like she carried a balloon inside.

When Tim came into the living room Tiffany faced him. "Why didn't you tell her what happened?" she asked.

"I'd be in big trouble," Tim answered. "And you promised," he reminded.

"I didn't tell," she said.

"Thanks!" Tim reached over and grabbed Tiffany's hand as he spoke. His eyes were so blue, so earnest as he looked at Tiffany, that she couldn't stay angry. But she also couldn't keep the secret inside. It hurt too much.

"I have to tell," she said. "I have to know why. I have to talk to Mom and Dad."

Tim's eyes widened. "But, you promised," he said again.

"I know." Tiffany felt the unfairness of it all wrenching the lump inside of her stomach. Her eyes filled again, willing him silently to understand. "Can we tell her together?" she asked.

A long moment passed. Then, Tim nodded.

Tiffany swallowed hard as he took her hand.

Snapping off the television with her free hand, she trailed him down the hallway to the kitchen where Mom would be waiting.

four

Mom was putting the caps on jars of warm strawberry jam when Tiffany and Tim entered the kitchen. "Did you two decide to make up?" she asked.

Tiffany nodded.

Slipping the last jar of jam into the canning pot on the stove, Mom placed the lid on top and turned to face them. "Do you want to tell me about it?"

The crooked letters on Mom's apron seemed to jump out at Tiffany and she nodded again as she traced each letter with her eyes . . . M . . . O . . . M. . . .

It was Tim who spoke first. "I said something I shouldn't have," he said, the nerves making his voice crack.

"Oh?" Mom said. "Was it something that hurt your sister's feelings?"

Tiffany looked up, the tears brimming in her eyes. "Am I adopted?" she blurted out.

Shock registered on Mom's face. Then a bewildered look, replaced by one of sadness. She sank into a kitchen chair and pulled Tiffany close. Resting her head on Tiffany's shoulder, she whispered, "Oh, I wanted to tell you when the time was right." Then, "Yes. You are."

"Why didn't you tell me?"

Mom pulled Tiffany onto her lap and stroked her hair. "We weren't sure when you should know.

We just didn't know."

"But Tim knew," Tiffany accused. "You told him!"

"I didn't," Mom said. "I didn't know Tim knew."

Tim slid into a chair beside them and stared at his folded hands. "I was four years old, Mom," he said. "I knew. I still remember when Tiffany came."

Mom looked at Tim with surprise. "You do?"

"Sure! She had on that little pink dress with letters on the front. Her hair was sticking out from under a bonnet. I remember thinking, Wow, she has red hair!"

"I just didn't know," Mom repeated. "I didn't think you understood what adoption was."

"I *was* four," Tim repeated.

Mom turned to Tiffany. Pulling her close she said, "We did adopt you, but it was because we wanted a daughter so, so very much. And when I first saw you . . . just after you were born, I fell in love with you. I knew deep inside that you truly *were* my daughter. It has always been that way. I even forget that I didn't give birth to you." Mom paused. "Your birth mother couldn't care for you. She was much too young. But we needed you, and wanted you so much. We brought you home from the hospital just after you were born."

Tiffany had expected to be angry or hurt, but she felt none of that now. What she felt was loved . . . and wanted.

But Tim looked as if he were about to cry. "I didn't mean to tell Tiffany," he said softly. "Really, I didn't."

Mom reached across the table to Tim and patted his hand. "It's okay," she said. "Tiffany had to know some day."

Looking at Tiffany, her eyes searching, she said, "Do you understand that it doesn't matter who gives birth to you . . . that I am your *real* mother?" she asked.

Tiffany hugged her mom. "Yes," she said.

Later that night, lying in bed, Tiffany's thoughts raced. The kitchen talk had helped her feel better, but she still felt different. It was almost as if she were a shell now. She still lived inside of Tiffany Clark's body. But she wasn't sure who she *really* was. She felt like an outsider, looking in. How long would it be, she wondered, until she could feel like herself again?

All at once Tiffany remembered Windy and Mr. Paul's invitation for her to help him with the ponies. She sat up in bed. Downstairs she could hear her mom and dad talking over the hum of the television. She hopped out of bed and headed down the steps. Some things could not wait until morning and this was one of them.

Mom was lying on her side on the couch, covered by an afghan, watching television. Dad sat by her feet reading a book under the glow of the lamp. They looked up when she came in.

"Hi, puddin'," Dad said, using the pet name he hadn't used since she was very small. "What's up?"

She sat on the couch in front of her mom. "I forgot to tell you something today. After Tim and I argued, I walked down to the pony farm to pet the ponies." She paused, fiddling with the corner of the afghan.

"I used to go there when I was little," Mom said wistfully.

"Mr. Paul told me!" Tiffany was excited now and her voice rose. "He said you used to help him with the ponies. He asked me if I wanted to help with them too!"

Mom sat up, pulling the afghan with her as she rose. "I don't know, Tiffany. You don't know horses that well. It's not like you've been around them much. . . ."

"Dad?" Tiffany looked to her father for support. "I'm not a baby anymore!"

"I know, puddin'. But your Mom worries. It's her job to worry," he said. Then he smiled.

Tiffany didn't see the humor. "Mom!" she wailed. "You did it when you were my size. Mr. Paul said so!"

"I was raised with ponies," Mom said. "I knew how to handle them."

"Well, I can learn," Tiffany said firmly. Her chin

came up. "I'll be careful and I'll go slow. Please?"

Mom looked at Dad again. "Paul is good with kids as well as horses," she said to him, and then for a moment it was as if Tiffany wasn't even in the room, as if they were speaking without talking. Then she saw her father nod lightly.

"My favorite pony, Windy, is going to have a foal soon." Tiffany said. "I want to be there when she does."

"That is exciting," Dad said.

A thoughtful expression crossed Mom's face. "I don't know . . ." she hesitated. "What if one of the ponies hurts you?"

"I won't get hurt! I told you I will be careful. You gotta trust me."

Dad put his hand on Tiffany's knee. "I think you're old enough," he said.

"Paul does have a nice bunch of ponies," Mom said.

Tiffany jumped up and hugged her mom, and then her dad. "Then it's settled, right? I can do it?"

"Yes," Mom said. "But remember your promise.

Be careful and take it slow until you know the ponies. Each one is a little different from the next. No two ponies are the same."

"I know," Tiffany said. "I already know that Windy is the best."

Later that night, Tiffany wrestled with sleep. Prancing ponies filled her thoughts. *Maybe*, she thought, *the ponies will help me figure out who I really am.*

five

Tiffany slid her legs into the car and pulled the door shut. Mom turned the key in the ignition and the car came to life.

"I could have walked," she said.

"I want to take you the first time," Mom answered. Backing out of the driveway, her eye in the rearview mirror, she continued, "I haven't seen Paul in quite some time. It will be nice to see him and the ponies." She glanced at Tiffany and her eyes held a sparkle. "I bet I know how you feel," she said.

Tiffany adjusted her seat belt and squirmed into a comfortable position. "What do you mean?"

"I remember how good it felt to see the ponies, to be with them, and oh . . . how good they smelled!"

Tiffany grinned in surprise and felt herself relax. Her mom remembered how wonderful the smell of a horse could be. She must have loved horses just as much when she was young.

Tiffany saw the wistful look on Mom's face. "Yeah," Tiffany agreed out loud. "They smell so . . . so . . . I don't know, warm and good!"

Mom's hand came across the car, grasping her daughter's knee. "We are so much alike," she said.

Tiffany looked down at Mom's hand. Like mother, like daughter, she thought wryly. But it *was* neat, knowing that Mom could share the same feelings.

At the farm, Paul greeted Tiffany with a booming "Hello!" and a pat on the back. But he wrapped

Mom in a bear-size hug. "It's been too long, Susan," he said. Then, seeing her eyes wander toward the pasture he grinned. "You miss them too," he said, indicating the ponies. "I can see it in your face. Do you miss them more than me?" he asked jokingly.

Mom laughed. "No. But they are still special."

Tiffany saw Windy off in the distance. She was grazing near the spot where Tiffany visited, pulling up the tufts of grass by the honeysuckle covered fence. Tiffany watched her a moment, then moved into the barn, down the aisle, checking out the stalls as she went along. She had never been inside of the barn. It was long and low with at least ten stalls on each side. Outside of each stall was a pile of wet and dirty straw bedding. Some of the stalls were empty, their back doors open to the pasture beyond. Others held short, stocky Shetland-type ponies with comical, fuzzy faces, or Chincoteague ponies, tall and graceful with Arabian dish faces.

Tiffany stopped to rub a black pony's velvety nose. She heard Mom talking with Mr. Paul, laughing from time to time. Their voices blended as Tiffany wandered down the aisle.

In the last stall, a tall, blonde-haired girl worked. She mucked out little piles of wet straw and manure with a pitchfork, dumping them outside the stall door in a bigger pile.

"Hi." the girl said when she saw Tiffany. "Are you Tiffany?"

Tiffany nodded, surprised to find the girl knew her name.

"I'm Mandy," the girl said. "Mr. Paul told me you would be here today."

"Oh," Tiffany said, not sure what to say next.

"What grade are you in?" Mandy continued to pick through the stall, removing bedding as she spoke.

"Fourth."

"I'm in fifth," Mandy said. "But I live over on the mainland so I don't go to Chincoteague Elementary School."

"Oh," Tiffany said, thinking the girl looked older.

"Hey, how about grabbing some of that straw and bringing it in here," the girl said.

Tiffany looked where the girl was pointing and saw four bales of bright yellow straw piled against the wall across the aisle. The top bale was already cut open and some of the straw had been removed. Now Tiffany pulled out a big armful of the crisp bedding and carried it into the stall. Carefully she scattered the straw, pulling apart the clinging sections, covering the bare spots in the stall floor. Just as she was finishing, the girl led a tiny grey and white pony into the stall. "This is Ghost," Mandy said. "He's a Falabello Miniature horse."

Tiffany scrubbed dirt from Ghost's neck and the pony turned his face to her. He seemed to be enjoying the rub. Tiffany kicked apart a few clumps of straw and followed Mandy out of the stall, latching the door securely behind her. Just then, Mom and Mr. Paul came down the aisle.

"Looks like Mandy's already got you started," Mr. Paul said. "Well, I'll leave you to it, then."

"I'm going to go now, too," Mom said. "I'll be back in a few hours to pick you up."

"Okay, Mom," Tiffany said as Mom gave her a quick hug.

From Ghost's stall, they moved on to the next stall and then the next. As Mandy cleaned out the wet, used straw and manure, piling it in the aisle, Tiffany cut open the bales of straw with a pair of old barn shears. She pulled arm load after arm load of straw from the bale and scattered it inside each stall. As they worked the girls talked, getting to know each other. Tiffany learned that Mandy was Mr. Paul's niece. She had been helping her Uncle Paul with the ponies for over a year now, and she'd been around them her whole life.

The girls talked and shoveled, piled and scattered fresh straw. By the time the stalls were done and they were forking the used bedding into wheel barrels to push outside, Tiffany felt like she had found a friend.

six

Tiffany fell into a pattern. Three days a week she worked for Mr. Paul, cleaning stalls, dumping cans of grain into the feed boxes for each pony and lugging buckets of water, too. On those days she talked to Mandy about who would foal first, Windy or Stormy, and which ponies were their favorites. They discussed school and home, horseback riding, and what they would do when they grew up. But Tiffany never told her secret. She was afraid to tell anyone, especially her new friend. She had wanted a friend to confide in so much and now her wish had come true. But still, she couldn't tell.

The other days of the week Tiffany helped Mom in the garden or kitchen, talked on the phone with Mandy, or wandered down the road just to visit the ponies. That was when she had her time alone with Windy.

Windy was her confidant, the only one she could trust with all of her secrets, and she didn't hold back. She told Windy how it felt to be alone even when you were with your family. And how she still wasn't sure if she fit in, even though she knew Mom and Dad loved her very much, and that even Tim did too, despite all his teasing. He loved her, in his big-brother way. But she wasn't a real Clark.

Sometimes she wondered if the woman who gave birth to her had long red hair and blue eyes. Who was she and where did she live? And most of all, why didn't she keep her baby girl? And what about her dad? Questions like that crept upon Tiffany. They came to her at night when she tried to sleep. Then, in the daytime, she talked to Windy about all of it.

Windy listened like no one else. She rubbed her head against Tiffany, up and down her arm, nearly knocking Tiffany off of her feet. She snorted from time to time. She stood quite still to be scratched. But she never talked back. She never said, "Stop asking yourself those questions. You have a family and that's all that matters." She never said, "Why does it matter if you are adopted?" Or, "Be grateful for the family that you *DO* have." Tiffany guessed that's what people would say if she asked those questions out loud. But not Windy.

Windy just loved her, no matter what secrets she shared, no matter what questions she asked. To Tiffany, the mare's love was like a promise, a promise that things would be better.

Each day Windy grew larger and larger. Her belly was like a barrel, bulging with the unborn foal.

Stormy was growing, too. But, Stormy was an indifferent little pony . . . not as friendly as Windy. Stormy was lightly shorter than Windy, but she was a brown and white pinto, too. She was not mean, or nasty. She did not kick or bite. But she was not loving either. When it came to people, she could either take them or leave them. She had grown up in the spotlight and she took all that attention for granted.

Windy was a people pony. She loved attention, and Tiffany knew that she loved *her* too. So it was Windy she watched the closest. It was Windy she stroked and kissed. It was Windy's mane that she braided and unbraided, twisted and finger combed. It was Windy she loved and watched and waited with.

But it was Stormy who foaled first.

It happened on a hot night in early July. Tiffany was at home when the phone rang.

"Hello," Tiffany said.

"Hey, Tif?"

"Yes. Who is this?"

"It's Mandy, you goof! See if you can come down to the farm."

Tiffany could hear the excitement rising in Mandy's voice. "Why? What's going on?" Then after just a second the excitement rose in her own voice. "Did Windy have her foal?"

"No. But Stormy is foaling now. Hurry and get down here!"

"Is it born yet?"

"No. She just went down in her stall a few minutes ago. Mr. Paul said to call you . . . that you'd want to be here. He said to tell your mom to come, too."

"How long? I mean, will we get there in time to see it?"

"I don't know." Mandy's voice seemed impatient. "Look, I gotta go. I don't want to miss it. Just hurry up. Okay?"

"Yes!" Tiffany nearly shouted. "I'll be there soon." Tiffany dropped the receiver into its cradle and hurried into the living room. "Mom!" she yelled. "Mom!"

seven

By the time Mom and Tiffany arrived at the farm, Stormy had already given birth. The new foal was a brown and white pinto just like her mother, and it was a female. The filly was lying on its side in the straw, trying to lift her head to see the world around it. Mr. Paul rubbed the foal with a rag, drying the matted wet hair with each stroke. Stormy was standing at the hay rack, munching hay as if she didn't have a care in the world.

"Is she alright?" Tiffany asked. She leaned over the stall door to watch. Mom stood behind her.

Mr. Paul looked up and immediately Tiffany could see that worry etched his face. "So far she's okay," he said. "But something's not right. Stormy didn't clean her up. She hasn't even touched her."

"She barely even looked at her," Mandy added from behind them.

Tiffany spun around. "Mandy! Thanks for calling me. Did you get to see the birth?"

"Yes." Mandy said it dully, no excitement lighting her voice.

Then the full meaning of what was happening hit Tiffany. She felt her mom wrap an arm around her shoulder. "What will happen to the foal?" Mom whispered.

Mr. Paul seemed to crumble. Sitting back in the straw he stroked the tiny head. "I don't know," he answered. "Some foals respond to foal formula . . . bottle feedings. But some don't. If Stormy doesn't start paying attention to this little one soon . . ." He paused again, wiping his brow with the rag before continuing. "She may not make it," he finished.

Tiffany buried her face in her mom's sleeve and fought back the tears that threatened to appear. She looked at the filly again. The face was brown with a patch of white. Her eyes were big and liquid brown. They were lined with thick black eyelashes that brushed her face as soft as feathers when she closed them. The filly looked up at Mr. Paul once more, then layed her head in his lap and closed those big brown eyes.

"We have to help her . . ." Tiffany said.

"Let's give them some space," Mr. Paul said. "Maybe Stormy will pay attention to her daughter if they're left alone."

Something about the way Mr. Paul said it made Tiffany grab hold of her mother's hand. "Is this her first baby?" Tiffany asked.

"This is Stormy's fifth foal," Mr. Paul said. "She's never done this, though." He slipped the filly's head into the warm bedding and stood. Brushing the straw from his pants, he opened the door as Tiffany stepped back. "She's always taken care of her foals before," he said more to himself than to anyone else. "I don't know what has gotten into her."

Mr. Paul slipped through the stall door, then shut and latched it behind him. "Let's go have a soda. Maybe if they are alone for a little while . . ." His voice trailed off as he headed down the aisle. Mom patted him on the shoulder as he passed and Mandy and Tiffany fell into step behind the two adults.

They returned to the stall a half hour later. Stormy was standing at the hay rack in the opposite corner from the filly. Her head drooped into the uneaten hay as she dozed.

The filly was still on her side in the same position they had left her in. Her eyes were shut and she was as still as the night itself. Each breath barely lifted her ribs, up and down, up and down.

"Enough of this," Mr. Paul boomed in a voice so loud it made Tiffany jump and Stormy's eyes fly open. "This little filly has got to have some nourishment." He moved into the stall. Slipping his arms under the newborn he picked her up. The filly opened her eyes wide and began to scramble, waving her legs in the air, seeking contact with the ground. A moment later she was standing with help from Mr. Paul. He steadied the foal beside Stormy, guiding her nose toward the warm milk of the mare's udder.

Stormy snorted and laced her ears back. She side-stepped away from the foal and lifted a hind leg as if threatening to kick.

"No you don't!" Mr. Paul warned the mare. He laid a hand across her rump. The tone of his voice and the firm touch calmed Stormy, but it was plain to see she didn't like what was going on.

Finally, the filly found the warm milk bag and she began to suckle, weak at first and then stronger. Her mouth steadily pulled forth the nourishment she needed to live.

Mr. Paul had to remind Stormy to behave again and again. She didn't want anything to do with her foal, but she seemed to know she didn't have a choice. When the foal was full she began to play with the milk, letting it run from her mouth in rivulets, then sucking again. She looked around the room in between spells of sucking, and she seemed to take in everything she saw. Her eyes were intense as she stared, moving from one person to another.

"Okay, little girl," Mr. Paul said softly. "You've had enough." He led the foal away from Stormy. "Open that door for me, will you?" he asked.

Mandy unlatched the door and swung it wide.

"It's plain to see that Stormy doesn't want her little girl," he said sadly. "So we'll just put her in the next stall down. She'll be able to see her momma but Stormy won't be able to hurt her."

Hurt her? Could Stormy hurt her own baby? "Would she do that?" Tiffany asked.

"I don't know," Mr. Paul said. "But I'm not taking any chances. She sure isn't thrilled about this one." He rubbed the filly's nose, then lifted her in his arms and carried her out into the aisleway.

"Would you girls get that empty stall ready for her?" he asked.

Already Mandy was dragging a bale of straw down the aisle and into the stall. She cut it open with the shears and Tiffany jumped in, grabbed some straw, and scattered it on the dry floor. She and Mandy used the whole bale, making it extra deep. The little filly would need to stay warm and feel safe. She had no mother to snuggle up against, no warm touch to settle her. The straw would have to be soft and comforting.

Carefully, Mr. Paul carried the newborn into the stall. He put her down in the straw. It came up to her knees. The pinto reached down and touched it with her nose, rooting for a moment. Then her knees buckled and she sank into the bedding, stretching out and resting her head in it. As she closed her eyes, Mr. Paul shooed them from the stall and closed the door. "Let her rest," he said.

"Will she be okay?" Tiffany asked again.

"Don't know." His answer was quick and short, but then he looked down at Tiffany and his hand fell to her shoulder. "Honestly, it doesn't look good, Tiffany," he said. "Stormy doesn't want this one. I could make her nurse it tonight, but she's still weak from giving birth. When she gets stronger, she might not let me do that. She might not ever let that little filly nurse again."

Tiffany dropped back behind Mom and Mr. Paul. Falling into step with Mandy, their eyes locked and she could see the same worry reflected in Mandy's eyes that she felt inside.

Late that night, Tiffany lay in her bed as still as the night itself. It was hot and sticky and humid and Tiffany felt the same way inside. All clogged up. *How could a mother reject her own baby?* Then a chilling thought came over her. The same thing had happened to her.

eight

The next day Tiffany walked the road to the pony farm alone. The day was as humid as the night had been, and the sun shone through a fuzzy haze. She stomped at the tar bubbles rising in the road and thought about the foal. Poor little thing, all alone in a big new world. *She* was lucky, Tiffany decided about herself. Even if the woman who gave birth to her hadn't wanted her, she had a real mother waiting to take her. Stormy's filly was all alone.

Mandy was already at the farm when Tiffany arrived. It seemed as if she was always there. She was hanging over the stall door, watching the filly. It was standing in a corner of the stall, looking lost in a sea of yellow straw.

"How is she?" Tiffany asked.

"Stormy wouldn't let her nurse," Mandy said. "Mr. Paul tried some formula, but she didn't get much. Most of it just ran out of her mouth and she wouldn't swallow it."

Tiffany saw a can as big as a paint can sitting by the stall. It said Foal-Lac on its side. "That?" she asked.

"Yea," Mandy answered. "It's a powder. Mr. Paul mixed it with warm water and gave it to her in a bottle. She didn't like it though."

Tiffany remembered having once tasted powdered milk. "I don't blame her," she said. "Powder mixed with water . . . yuck!" She looked at the filly again.

Her head was hanging, almost to her knees. She looked so dejected.

Tiffany opened the stall door and slipped inside. She dropped beside the tiny pinto. The baby lifted her head and rested it on Tiffany's shoulder, whuffing warm breaths into Tiffany's ear. She wrapped her arms around the newborn and buried her head in her fuzzy coat. "You poor thing," she whispered again.

"I feel the same way," Mandy said softly. "Mr. Paul said this one is almost marked like Misty, her grandmother. She's not the same color as Misty, but she still looks like her in many ways. He might name the filly Misty II," Mandy added.

"Misty II," Tiffany whispered softly. It seemed to fit the tiny filly. She was soft and fuzzy-looking, like mist.

All at once, Mr. Paul came barreling down the aisle. "Girls! Come quick," he shouted. "Windy's down. She's going to foal at any minute!"

Tiffany jumped up, patting the filly. Then she hurried out of the stall. Mandy sprinted from the barn behind Mr. Paul and Tiffany followed. She saw Windy on the other side of the pasture, on her side, lying under the big maple tree. Her breath caught in her throat at the sight of her favorite mare lying down. "Please," she whispered. "Let everything go okay. Let Windy and the foal be alright." Her thoughts finished her wish. *And make Windy want her foal. Make her love it.*

Mr. Paul had some soft rags, a bucket of warm water and a bottle of iodine. He knelt down beside Windy's head. "You're alright," he said. "We'll take good care of you."

Mandy stood behind Mr. Paul and Tiffany knelt behind Windy's neck. She smoothed the strands of long mane in her hand. "Good girl," she said quietly. Then she leaned to whisper in Windy's ear. "I'm here now," she said. Windy rolled her eyes to look up at Tiffany, as if she knew it was okay now. Then she snorted.

Tiffany watched as the mare's stomach tightened

again and again. It wasn't long until the foal slid from her, front hooves first, followed by the head with a little muzzle almost resting on the front hooves. Then came the shoulders, and all of it wrapped in a shroud. Like the sheer white curtains that hung from Tiffany's bedroom windows, a transparent veil covered the newborn.

Tiffany held her breath and watched as the foal broke the shroud with a front hoof and a muzzle.

Windy turned to look at her new foal curiously. Then it seemed like only a few minutes before Windy struggled to stand, tearing the shroud. Tiffany and Mandy each followed Mr. Paul's lead, moving back quietly and watching.

Windy lowered her nose to the ground and nosed her newborn foal softly. She snorted, pushing away the remainder of the sac. She licked her foal's face with a long swipe of her tongue. Then another and another. The little one's eyes were already open and it gazed at its mother trance-like.

"It's a boy!" Mr. Paul said softly as the colt began to thrash his legs like a windmill. "He's like a little cyclone!"

A moment later the colt was struggling to stand.

Tiffany gasped. "He's already trying to stand up. Is that okay?" She looked to Mr. Paul.

Mr. Paul's face was split with a grin and he was nodding and rubbing his spiky hair. "You bet it is. This is how a foaling is supposed to go!"

Windy licked and nosed her new son, urging him along. He would get halfway up, stumble forward, then fall to the ground again. Sometimes he went backward, his legs pedaling for all their worth, seeking balance, then losing it and crumbling to the ground again. Each time he tried to stand he fell, but he didn't give up.

Tiffany and Mandy watched side by side while Mr. Paul leaned against the trunk of the maple. Tiffany was surprised when she felt Mandy's hand grasp her own. She looked at her new friend and grinned.

She felt like she was struggling with the colt and

falling with him. She wished and willed for him to make it to his feet, and soon the colt *was* standing, wobbling unsteadily beside his momma. Windy nuzzled him gently, pushing him toward the milk, and then he was nursing, sucking in great gulps, his eyes closed contentedly, his whole body rocking with the motion of his sucking.

Tiffany felt tears well in her eyes. First, watching the birth and now this . . . it was more wonderful than anything she had ever seen. She looked at Mr. Paul and Mandy. Mandy's eyes were as full as her own, threatening to spill tears of joy. Mr. Paul was rubbing his hair again, all smiles and sparkle.

"Guess I don't need this," he said, indicating the bucket and rags. "She's cleaning him off on her own."

Sure enough, Windy was scrubbing the newborn clean with her long, rough tongue. Lovingly and gently she introduced herself to her son.

"And God took a handful of southerly wind, blew his breath over it and created the horse," Mr. Paul said.

"What's that?" Mandy asked.

"It's a Bedouin legend," he said. "I think of it every time I see a foal come into the world."

Tiffany watched the tiny foal, another brown and white pinto. This one had a lot more white on its sides than Stormy's filly and his back was completely white. But the triangle of white on the left side of his neck just under the top of the mane was just the same, and so was the wide white blaze that ran down his face. The wind ruffled the scrubby fluff of mane along his neck and Mandy could see where the Bedouin legend might have come from. The colt was so beautiful, like the wind and everything natural. Only God's breath could have created something so perfect.

Mr. Paul moved forward and Windy lowered her nose to be scratched. She rolled her eyes toward the colt, then back at Mr. Paul. She seemed proud of her new son and both girls giggled at her antics.

Mr. Paul used a swab to brush some iodine on the underbelly of the new foal. "It keeps infection out," he explained at Tiffany's puzzled look. "Come on, girls," he said, gathering up the bucket and rags. "It's time to leave these two to themselves. We've got barn chores to do."

Reluctantly, Tiffany followed Mr. Paul and Mandy from the field. She watched Windy one more time before leaving. The mare was licking the colt's neck and the colt was nursing by her side.

Later that day, Tiffany followed Mr. Paul back to the pasture. The stalls were clean and the feed bins filled. There was fresh hay in each stall along with clean buckets of water. Before Mandy's mom had picked her up to go home the girls had prepared a stall for Windy and her new colt next to Stormy's filly. "If she can see the new colt, maybe she'll feel less alone," Mandy had said, and Mr. Paul had agreed.

Windy came to them as soon as they entered the pasture. The newborn trotted alongside her. "Look at him go," Tiffany said. "You sure were right when you said he was like a cyclone," she said, seeing the power in his legs as they carried him by his mother's side.

"By golly," Mr. Paul said as he clipped a lead shank to Windy and led her inside. "I believe that's a perfect name for this little one. We'll call him Cyclone."

Tiffany laughed. Cyclone followed Windy into the stall. Stormy's frail filly watched through the wooden rails with a look of curiosity. She stumbled forward, shoving her nose over the rail. Then a weak, high pitched squeal rang out. It was the first sound the filly had ever made other than sniffing and sucking. Windy's head shot up at the sound. She peered over the rail at the filly, her own colt sidestepping tight against her.

Tiffany saw Windy's big brown eyes roll toward the filly and she felt hope spring up inside of her. "She likes the filly," she half whispered, half spoke.

Mr. Paul smiled and nodded. "She might just take this one."

"What do you mean?" Tiffany asked.

"She might be willing to adopt the filly, too.

Sometimes a mare will take care of another mare's foal. Sometimes they won't. But, the good ones will do it."

Tiffany felt tears spring to her eyes for the second time that day and hope filled her. The filly would have a chance now, because Windy was definitely one of the good ones. Tiffany knew it as well as she knew Windy herself. The filly would finally have a chance at life.

nine

"Wake up, Tiffany," Mom whispered. "Get up." Tiffany's eyes flew wide. "What? What is it? Mom?" she asked. She sat up in bed, rubbing her eyes. The sun cast a grey pall into the room. Her alarm clock read 6 A.M.

"Mr. Paul called. He wants to know if you can come."

Tiffany scrambled from the bed, throwing off her nightgown and pulling open dresser drawers as she spoke. "What's wrong? Is it Windy? Why does he want me this early?"

"Calm down, honey," Mom said. "Mr. Paul said the filly is weak. He wants to try her with Windy, but he wants you there, first. He said you have a way with Windy. He said you calm her . . . that you two share a bond."

Despite her worry, what Mom said warmed her. She knew she shared a bond with Windy, but she didn't know anyone else had noticed. She pulled jeans from her bottom drawer and a t-shirt from another. Mom shut the drawers behind her daughter and smoothed her hair after the t-shirt was on.

Tiffany hurried to wash her face and brush her hair while Mom hovered nearby. "Do you want to go?" she asked her mom through a mouthful of foaming toothpaste.

"Sure. I'd like that," Mom said. "I'll drive us over so you can get there quicker."

They found Mr. Paul in little Misty II's stall. He had the rag again, scrubbing the foal's neck and legs softly. She wasn't wet, but she needed the love and attention. Tiffany knew that. Windy was pacing in her stall next door, her colt curled up in a corner, sleeping soundly. She rubbed her muzzle over the bars that separated the filly from her, watching.

"She took a little more Foal-Lac last night and a little this morning," Mr. Paul said of Misty II. "But it just isn't enough to keep her going. Stormy won't even let her near. But Windy's been carrying on, mooing like a cow at her all morning."

At the mention of her name, Windy rubbed her muzzle over the bars again, and a soft moaning moo escaped her lips. It wasn't the whinny or the neigh that Tiffany was accustomed to hearing. It *did* sound like a cow's moo! But it was soft and gentle and full of concern.

"See what I mean?" Mr. Paul said. "I thought as long as she was acting like that we ought to try putting these two together."

Tiffany nodded and reached for Windy. Windy leaned over the stall door and burrowed her head in Tiffany's shirt. "There, there," Tiffany said softly. "Are you worried about that little one?"

Windy's head rose and she searched Tiffany's face as if she needed an answer to some unasked question. Then she went back to pacing and stopping to stare through the bars at Misty II.

"Do you want to lead her in with Misty II?" Mr. Paul asked. "I'll help the filly up if you think you can handle Windy."

"Sure I can. She's my buddy. Aren't you girl?" she asked the mare, and Windy pressed her head into Tiffany's jacket in reply. Tiffany reached up to unclip the lead shank that hung by the door. She hooked it onto Windy's halter. While Mom held the door open wide, she led the mare out and into the next stall.

Mr. Paul held Misty II up. "Before we try this I better tell you a few things," he said. "Windy might not be as thrilled about this as we all hope she'll be. If she starts to nip or kick or anything crazy, you just get her out of here and let me worry about the filly. Okay?"

Tiffany nodded. She couldn't imagine Windy doing anything like that, but she would be careful just the same.

Slowly, Mr. Paul brought the filly to meet Windy. Windy's eyes had not left the filly's face, and now she snorted her pleasure and stretched her neck to meet the little pinto. All of Tiffany's worries were cast aside when Windy began to wash the white blaze that ran down the tiny face. The mare's tongue was so big and rough that Misty II would have been knocked off of her feet had Mr. Paul not been there to help. Windy nosed Misty II, shoving her tiny body back and toward the milk.

It was only a moment until the filly was nursing. Windy stood as still as a statue, watching the newborn for a few moments. Then she resumed licking and scrubbing, absorbing the scents of her new daughter, fulfilling a pony promise.

Tiffany felt Mom's arm come around her as they watched it all. Noisily, Misty II rooted and suckled with all of her might. Her tail switched from side to side and her whole body swayed with the motion of it all. Mr. Paul unclipped the lead shank from Windy's halter and the three of them filed from the stall.

"She's a good one," Mr. Paul said.

"Looks like she's got a new baby daughter," Mom added, and her arm gripped Tiffany's shoulder even more tightly.

As they watched the mare and the filly, Tiffany's thoughts turned to her mom. Windy was a lot like her own mom, Tiffany thought. She was strong and loving. She was quiet when Tiffany needed someone to listen, and she was there when Tiffany needed someone to hug. That is what a *real* mother is all about, Tiffany thought.

It's not who gives birth to you, but who is there when you are sick and in need, like the filly. It's not who gives birth to you, but who really cares.

Suddenly Tiffany realized that she *was* a Clark after all. She was a Clark in the most important way. She belonged.

As she watched Windy nurse the little filly, Tiffany realized that, even in nature, there are real mothers, and mothers who can't always care for their young. Even animals adopt, Tiffany thought, and it surprised her.

Wrapping her arms around her mom's waist, Tiffany hugged her tight.

A moment later Cyclone was awake and nickering for his momma. Mr. Paul led the little colt next door to meet his new sister. The filly had finished nursing and looked up expectantly at the colt as he charged inside. Windy lowered her head to greet her son, then took turns licking each one. She rumbled with satisfaction as she watched her new family. Tiffany smiled, feeling the same satisfaction deep inside.

AUTHOR'S NOTE

While this story is fictionalized, the characters of
Misty, Stormy, Windy, Cyclone, and Misty II are
based on real Chincoteague ponies. Windy did give
birth to a colt named Cyclone at about the same time
her mother Stormy gave birth to the filly, Misty II.
Stormy rejected her new foal, although there is some
debate about whether it was at birth, or shortly there-
after. Windy adopted Stormy's foal and raised it
alongside of her own.

Today Windy and Cyclone reside in Waynesboro,
Pennsylvania. Windy is the oldest living Misty
descendant. Misty II lives in Manheim, Pennsylvania,

and has become a successful show pony. Stormy died peacefully on a farm in Waynesboro, Pennsylvania just before Thanksgiving of 1993. She was thirty-one years old.

Paul Merritt still owns and operates the Misty Museum on Chincoteague Island in Virginia, where this story takes place.

*For more charming ponies
and a collectible pony charm don't miss:*

Turn the page for a sneak peek!

one

Niki Crawford jumped out of the pickup truck almost before it had even stopped. Horses and riders milled about on the edge of the parking lot, and a long, blue horse trailer was backing up to a ramp that led into the stockyard. Floodlights lit the whole area, including the white letters on the side of the building that read LIVESTOCK AUCTION.

"Wait up, Niki!" Dad puffed as he slid out of the driver's seat. "Those horses aren't going anywhere without you."

Niki turned and grinned at her dad, her dark eyes twinkling. He was older than most of her friends' fathers, but the thinning gray hair and the slight limp didn't bother Niki. He was still "good ol' Dad." They had been on their own for as long as Niki could remember. Her mother had died when Niki was young.

Slowing her step, she waited for her father. She felt for the lump of rolled money in her back pocket, running her hand over it to make sure it was still there. A ripple of nervous jitters ran through her. *Tonight's the night*, she thought. *I'm finally going to get my own horse.*

Dad put a hand on Niki's long dark hair, and they walked inside together. "Nervous?" he asked, and she nodded.

"I can't believe it's finally happening," she said out loud.

"You earned it," Dad answered matter-of-factly. "That was the deal. You earn it. You pay for it. You take care of it." He paused. "The hard part's ahead of you."

Niki frowned as she looked into her Dad's blue eyes. "You know I'll take care of it. I've wanted a horse for so long . . ." her voice trailed off; then she added softly, "I can't wait to take care of it."

Inside the auction barn Dad stopped to talk to old friends, and Niki wandered down the aisles. They had come here every Saturday night since Niki was little. Dad came to visit with friends from neighboring farms. Niki came for the horses.

Inside the ring, she heard the auctioneer beginning to sell the tack. She knew they would sell the saddles and bridles, brushes and tools for at least another hour before the horses and ponies were led in.

As Niki came to the first row of horses, she stopped to evaluate each one. She was looking for the perfect pony, the pony of her dreams. Would it be a chestnut or a bay, a pinto or a gray? It didn't matter to Niki what color it was. What mattered was something else. Maybe a certain look in its eye or the way it carried itself. Heck, she wasn't even quite sure what it would be. But she was sure that she would know it when she saw her special horse. She would just know.

In the first square pen was a tall, chestnut thoroughbred with two white stockings. He paced from side to side and threw back his head, his eyes rolling wildly. Sticking her head through the top two rails, Niki peered up at the chestnut. All at once he drew himself up and let out a loud whinny. Niki jumped so quick that she bumped her head on the top rail.

She rubbed her head as she moved on to the next pen. There she looked in at a tiny pinto mare with a young foal at its side. A crowd was already gathering around this pen, and Niki knew that the pair would bring a high price. She called it the "cute factor." Whenever there was a fuzzy or cute or young pony, the crowd would "ooh" and "ahh" and the animals would sell for a high price. She moved on.

❀ 4 ❀

Down the row she looked at a sturdy bay pony saddled in Western gear. He looked like a nice pony, but not special. She studied a dapple gray yearling for quite some time. It seemed sensitive enough, but it would be another year until she could ride it. There were two pintos—a tall, rangy looking sorrel and a stocky blood bay. Nothing special. Niki was beginning to get discouraged.

She'd worked so hard this summer, helping on the farm, earning the money the hard way, like Daddy said she had to, and now . . . where was her pony?

Turning back to the blue trailer, Niki watched as the driver and his partner returned from the business office to unload their cargo. The first one off was a magnificent black-and-white pinto with a flowing black tail. Niki felt her heart pound as she watched it come down the aisle, right past her and into a holding pen. But if she was impressed with the pinto, she was totally unprepared for the next one.

Her breath caught in her throat as she watched a pure white mare come off the trailer and down the ramp. The mane hung in long silvery strands and she held her head high. She was calm, Niki noticed. That was a trait she was looking for. But there was even more. A large pony, the mare was just the right height. She picked her hooves up daintily as she stepped through the dirty stockyard, almost as if it was not quite clean enough for her.

"Princess," Niki mumbled. The pony was an absolute princess. Then it came down the aisle right beside her, and Niki felt her heart explode as the mare tossed her head. By the time they had closed the gate of the holding pen, Niki was really excited. She reached back to feel the money in her pocket and she knew it would be enough. "Princess" was the one.

When the men had penned her and the vet had finished drawing blood from her neck for the required health check, Niki sidled closer. The man who had led the mare down the ramp and into the pen was a cowboy with a wide-brimmed hat. Now, as he left the pen, he slapped a sticker on the mare's rump: 56. Princess was number 56. It etched itself into

Niki's brain. The number she needed to bid on would be 56. The cowboy grinned at her. "She's a good one, little miss," he said, and Niki blushed. Was it so obvious that she was taken with the mare?

After the men had left, Niki clucked to the mare and she came right over. The face was long and dish-shaped, like an Arabian, with a tiny teacup nose and wide, deep-set eyes. They were soft and brown and they watched Niki closely as she reached through the rails to pat the horse on the shoulder. Without hesitation, the mare lowered her head and her velvety muzzle settled into Niki's hand. *With a spiraled horn she could be a unicorn from a fairy tale*, Niki thought.

There was a commotion behind her and a high-pitched whine rang out. "I want that one, Mamma! You gotta git me that one over there!"

A heavyset woman with rosy cheeks and a big stain on the front of her too tight T-shirt was coming down the aisle. With her hand clasped firmly in his, she was fairly dragging along a chubby little boy with a crew cut. But the whine had not come from the small child. It had come from nine-year-old Billy Baily. Niki knew him. He was in her class at school and he was a royal pain. Now he was pointing at her Princess.

Then he caught sight of Niki. "Hey! It's Niiiiki!" he crooned. "Icky, picky, sticky, Niki! Whatta you doin' here, Icky?"

Niki whirled around with her hands on her hips. "Same thing as you, Billy," she said. "It's a free country."

Instead of answering her Billy stuck his fingers in his ears and twirled them around, his tongue hanging out the side of his mouth and his eyes rolling up.

Niki turned and marched down the aisle, away from Billy and away from Princess. "Some people never grow up . . . Billy!" she said over her shoulder.

As Billy's whiney voice faded behind her, Niki hurried forward. There was a crowd gathered around another holding pen where a pony had just been unloaded. *Probably another "cute factor,"* she thought, but she knew she had to see for herself.

She heard the comment of a lady in front of her before she even saw the pony. "Poor, dear thing," the lady said under her breath.

After pushing her way through the sea of legs and bodies gathered around the rails, Niki knelt down and peered into the pen through the bottom rails. The pony was a little bit shorter than Princess, coal black with four white stockings and a narrow white blaze running down the length of his face. She could see his face clearly because it was hanging down to his knees, which were buckled from the sheer energy of holding himself up. Every rib protruded in agonizing detail and he heaved soft whuffing breaths. If it weren't for the way his spindley legs were braced, he would surely have been on the ground.

Niki's heart, which moments ago had danced with happiness, now dropped to her stomach. She fought a sick feeling that was oozing up from inside of her as she looked into the pony's glazed eyes.

"The doggers will buy this one for sure," she heard someone say and others grunted in agreement.

No! she thought angrily. How could they say that? How could they let the dog food buyers get him before he even had a chance? He had already suffered enough. Then, to die for that . . . to become canned dog food! It just wasn't fair.

Niki's hand snaked through the rails to stroke the pony's long white blaze. Slowly, the pony lifted his black head and met her gaze. He held her stare for a moment before dropping his head back down again. But that moment was all it took.

LOIS SZYMANSKI

is the author of many books for young readers. She lives in Westminster, Maryland, with her husband, two daughters, and three cats. She and her older daughter have four horses-one of them a Chincoteague pony named Sea Feather. When Lois isn't writing, she stays busy taking care of her family, talking to students in the classroom, and dreaming up new stories about horses.

YOU CAN VISIT LOIS ONLINE AT
www.angelfire.com/md/childauth/

A Pony to the Rescue

CHARMING PONIES

A Pony
to the
Rescue

LOIS SZYMANSKI

HarperFestival®
A Division of HarperCollinsPublishers

To Dan, a constant source of inspiration.

Acknowledgments

During the course of researching the legend of the lost Silver Mine of Silver Run, Maryland, I was privileged to find several resources that aided me. One was a column written by Ruth Seitler for *The Carroll County Times*. The other, a remarkable book entitled *Ghosts and Legends of Carroll County*, written by Jesse Glass and published by the Carroll County Public Library, offered immeasurable assistance. Parts of this book are quoted within the pages of *A Pony to the Rescue*. To both sources I wish to offer a special thank you.

A Pony to the Rescue

one

Crackling logs spit sparks from the flames of the bonfire. Shannon sat on her sled, yanked off her snow-soaked mittens, and placed them on a rock near the fire to dry. The moon was bright, casting its light eerily over the group of friends. Some sat on sleds, some on logs, warming their feet as they took a break from an evening of sledding.

Shannon threaded two marshmallows onto a stick and thrust them into the fire. "Do you want one?" she asked Amanda, holding the bag out to her friend.

Amanda took a marshmallow from the plastic bag, then passed it down the line to Ashley, Sharece, and Larry. Larry was the hired hand here on Christmas Tree Farm. Shannon's dad paid him to help with the daily chores of tree farming, and Larry came to work each day after school. He would graduate from high school this year and be off to college. Shannon knew she would miss him when he was away.

With Christmas just around the corner, this was the farm's busiest season. But there was still time for play. Larry had stayed after work to build a fire and join them for a sledding party. As Shannon's marshmallows caught fire, the others slid their own white puffs onto sticks for roasting.

"Ugghh!" Amanda exclaimed as Shannon blew out her marshmallows. Amanda stared at the blackened blobs on the end of the stick, then watched as Shannon blew on them one more time, then popped them into her mouth.

"Yuck! How can you eat them like that?" Amanda pushed her dark hair under her hat and grinned at her friend, brown eyes flashing.

"I like them that way!"

"My sister's weird," Ashley said, and everyone laughed except Shannon, who made a face at her little sister.

Ten inches of snow had fallen over the past week, bringing excitement to the valley of Silver Run. All day long, the kids had packed a path down the hill with their sleds, across the dormant cornfield, down to the pond. Then, Mom had brought marshmallows and hot chocolate and Dad had lit lanterns to line the sledding path. The moon was so bright the lamps really weren't needed, though. Nighttime sledding parties were the best, Shannon decided.

Larry sat silently, stirring the fire with a stick. The swaying branches of nearby trees made shadows dance all around him.

"Tell us a story," someone cried.

Shannon nudged Larry. "Tell us a *ghost* story," she added softly.

Larry looked at Shannon, then back into the fire before he spoke. "Do you kids know the legend of the lost silver mine of Silver Run?"

Shannon looked at Amanda. She was shaking her head no.

"I don't know that story," Shannon said.

"Me, either," Ashley chimed in. "Tell it, Larry! Tell it!"

"Tell us the legend," Sharece agreed. "Is it scary?"

"I'll let you decide," Larry said mysteriously. Then he leaned in toward the fire again. His blond bangs hung over his eyebrows as he stared straight ahead in silence. He pushed back his cap and began.

"A long time ago, a German man called Ahrwud lived near here, with his beautiful daughter, Frieda. Now, Ahrwud was a silversmith, and a good one, too. The things he crafted from silver brought customers from far and wide. Everyone wanted to buy a trinket, designed and made by Ahrwud. But his neighbors wondered about him. Every time they came to visit, Ahrwud was sleeping soundly in his bed, and this would be the middle of the day! When did he find time to make the beautiful silver spoons and candlesticks, jewelry and other things, if he slept so much?"

"Maybe he worked in his sleep!" Ashley joked, cutting the tension of the group.

"Ssshh!" everyone said at once. "Let Larry finish!"

"Frieda was young, but she kept the cabin clean, cooked the meals, and did the laundry. Her father left the cabin every night and usually didn't return until just before dawn. Often the local Indians came for him or brought him home again.

"Then, on Frieda's thirteenth birthday, Ahrwud came home with a beautiful brooch, cut from the finest silver. 'Happy Birthday!' he said as he handed her the piece.

❀ 5 ❀

"Frieda looked at the jewelry in her hand. It was oval with a pattern of cubic shapes cut into it so that it sparkled in the light when she turned it this way or that. Right in the center was a perfectly formed rose. It was surely the prettiest thing she had ever owned. She threw her arms around her father's neck and thanked him, then pinned the brooch to her worn apron.

"By noon the next day, Frieda could not contain her curiosity. Every time she looked at the beautiful brooch she wondered where it had come from. She just had to know! How had her father made such a beautiful piece? When did he find the time? Frieda began to wonder if all the townspeople's stories were true. So when Ahrwud awoke, she pleaded and begged with him to take her along that night. Ahrwud could not stand to see his beloved daughter so upset, so finally he gave in.

'I will take you to see the place where I get my silver and work it, but you cannot know where it is, so I will have to blindfold you!'

"Frieda was surprised that her father would blindfold her, but she agreed to do as he said. After her eyes were covered, Ahrwud grasped her hand, held a lantern high, and led her down a trail through the forests and fields. As they walked, Ahrwud told her about the silver mine.

"'My Indian friends have allowed me to use their sacred silver mine,' he told Frieda. 'But I have promised them I would never tell anyone else about it. They say if anyone else finds the mine, it will disappear and I will be severely punished. So you must keep this to yourself, my darling Frieda.'

"Frieda nodded her head solemnly, feeling the pull of the blindfold as she did. A moment later, her father closed a heavy door and removed the cloth from her eyes. Frieda was astonished at what she saw. They were in a giant cave. Its walls sparkled where veins of silver had been exposed. Piles of silver stones were in each corner of the room. A strong oak table was set up on one side and on it were many trinkets, brooches, pins, rings, and even a few candlesticks, some of them not yet finished. As Frieda watched, her father set to work on a piece of silver.

"Just before daybreak, Ahrwud blindfolded his daughter and led her home again. He made her repeat her promise to keep the secret. But Frieda wasn't sure she could keep this to herself, so on the way home, she broke the branches of bushes and trees, leaving a trail she could follow should she decide to return. Her father hurried her home, too preoccupied to see or hear what she had done.

"All day long, while Ahrwud slept, Frieda tossed and turned on her cot. Sleep would not come. She was filled with the excitement of what she had seen. Surely it wouldn't hurt to tell just one friend. So Frieda rose from her bed, bundled up, and hurried to visit with her friend Nina.

"It wasn't long before Nina and Frieda were following the trail of broken branches. Nina just had to see it for herself."

Larry straightened his back and took a deep breath. He stirred the dying embers, then added a log to the pile.

"That's not the end, is it?" Ashley protested.

"No," Larry said with a half smile. "You didn't want the fire to go out, did you?"

"Hurry! Finish the story," Amanda said.

Larry smiled again and leaned forward. As the new log caught, flames began to shoot high again and a faraway look came into Larry's eyes. Shadows filtered across the young man's face as he continued.

"It would have been okay if the girls had just looked and left," Larry said. "But you know how women can be!"

"Larry!" the girls scolded. "Come on!"

"Well, it's true. They couldn't just look and leave. Those two girls had to gather up sacks full of pure silver and even some half-finished trinkets, and take them along when they left. Breaking promises was dangerous back then, and it was a sure sign of trouble to come."

"What happened?" Sharece asked.

"That night the Indians came to Ahrwud's house for a final time. They dragged him and Frieda to the cave, and they were never seen again. But that wasn't all. The mine vanished, too, never to be found." Larry paused. "Only Nina lived to tell the story."

There was silence around the fire. Shannon thought about the silver mine and wondered if it was still in the hills, buried somewhere.

"Is this a true story?" she asked.

"They say it is," Larry said. "It happened up there." He motioned toward the hills. "Up on Rattlesnake Hill. And people say you should never visit Rattlesnake Hill at night. They say a big German man with a wide-brimmed hat wanders the hills after dark with a lantern glowing bright. Many have seen the ghost of Silver Run."

"Has anyone ever looked for the mine?" Amanda asked.

"Yes. Many have searched. Two have died. It is said that three men must die before the mine is found again."

Amanda whistled under her breath. The sound floated eerily into the night. Shannon grabbed Amanda's hand and they stared up into the hills, toward Rattlesnake Hill. The fire was dying down again and everything seemed to have a weird glow. Silver streaks of moonlight shone through the tree-tops.

"Who wants to make another run down the hill?" Ashley asked. She stood up, grabbing the rope on her sled.

Shannon looked down the long winding sled path, barely lit by the lantern's glow. "Not me!" she said.

"Me, either," Amanda agreed.

"I'm going inside," Sharece said.

Larry kicked snow over the fire. "I'll pick up the

lanterns on the path," he said. "You kids hurry on in. Shannon's mom is probably waiting."

As the girls trudged up the slope toward the old farmhouse, Larry turned down the hill. Shannon looked back at him. He was staring up toward the hills and she thought she saw a smile play across his lips.

two

Moonlight cut a cool, white path across the living room's hardwood floorboards. Shannon rolled over on her back, just out of reach of the light, and stared through the gap in the curtains into the night. Beside her, Amanda lay on her side, curled in her sleeping bag like a contented cat. On the other side of the room, Ashley and Sharece cuddled in their own cocoon of warmth, built by piling sleeping bags and blankets around themselves in a circle to block out the drafts. Amanda whistled softly through her nose as she slept, and Ashley mumbled meaningless words in her sleep, but Shannon was wide awake.

Somewhere out there in the cold moonlit night there was a silver mine, sealed away in secrecy. Somewhere out there a ghost could be floating over the hills, calling out for a soul who could not rest. Shannon kicked at her blankets and rolled to one side as the thoughts swirled in her head. Suppose the mine was really there? Suppose it was a treasure chest full of silver and trinkets? And just suppose . . . she could find it?

"Hey, you sleepyheads . . . it's time to get up!"

Shannon opened her eyes and pulled a strand of blonde hair off of her face. The curtains were still parted, but where the moonlight had entered at night, sunlight now cascaded into the room, bright and intense, reflecting off the snow outside.

Amanda crawled out of her sleeping bag, rubbing her eyes, her hair a mass of tumbled black curls. "I can't believe it's already morning," she groaned.

"Me, either," Shannon agreed.

"Morning always comes too early when you have a sleep-over party," Mom sympathized. "But every cloud has a silver lining, and today Dad's making breakfast," she added.

Across the room, Ashley bolted upright in her blankets. "Pancakes!" she squealed. "Is Daddy making Polish rolled pancakes?"

"You guessed it," Mom said.

"Mmmm." Shannon sat up. "Rolled pancakes. My favorite."

"What are they?" Amanda asked.

Ashley got a silly look on her face. "They're old pancakes we roll up around leftovers," she teased.

"No, they aren't!" Shannon scolded. "They're thin, and as big as the whole pan," she explained. "You roll them up with cinnamon or jelly. They're delicious!"

"I'm up!" Sharece suddenly said, and the growling

of her stomach could be heard all the way across the big living room.

As they hurried to the bathroom to brush their hair and teeth, Shannon could hear Dad banging around in the kitchen and her stomach began to rumble, too. Soon, they were all sitting around the big oak farm table, spreading cinnamon or jelly onto the golden circles and rolling them up to eat.

"Dad?" Shannon said as she bit into her pancake. "Id dare weally a wost silver mine?" She swallowed the mouthful and looked up expectantly.

"Don't talk with your mouth full," Dad reprimanded. Then he smiled. "Where did you hear about that?"

"Larry told us last night," Ashley answered.

Dad chuckled. "That boy loves to tell that story! I guess he had the hairs standing up on the backs of your necks!"

"Dad!" Shannon said impatiently. "Is there really a mine?"

"Well, I've always heard there was. The story has been around for as long as I've been around. Every town has a reason for its name and Silver Run is no different. The silver mine makes sense to me."

"But no one has ever found it?"

"Nope!"

The girls ate silently for a few moments, thinking about the silver mine, then Shannon had an idea. "Let's ride the horse up to Rattlesnake Hill today. We'll see if we can find anything."

"It's too cold," Ashley said as she shoveled in another bite.

"Yeah, Shannon," Sharece agreed, "and you only have one pony. Who gets to ride?"

Shannon grinned sheepishly. She was disappointed. It had seemed like a great idea to her.

"I'll go," Amanda said.

Shannon reached under the table and squeezed her best friend's hand. "We can ride doubleback."

❀ ❀ ❀

Christa waited patiently while Shannon pulled the girth around her belly. Her nostrils snorted warm clouds of air when she breathed. Shannon buckled the girth tightly to make sure the saddle stayed in place. She rubbed the thick white fur on the pony's side. Christa's winter coat felt warmer than an electric blanket.

Amanda rubbed Christa's nose gently as she waited. "You know," she said, "Christa blends right in with the snow. She's a great horse to use for spying . . . like winter camouflage!"

"Yeah!" Shannon agreed. "But we really aren't spying. There's no one up there anymore."

Amanda laughed mysteriously. "How do you know?"

Shannon felt a chill go through her at the thought of the ghosts of Ahrwud and Frieda watching them, or even worse, angry Indians! She pulled Christa's reins over her head. "Do you want the front or back?" she asked her friend.

"The back. I always feel better when I can hold on to your waist."

Shannon climbed up on the fence and slid into the saddle. She grabbed Amanda's mittened hand and pulled her up behind.

"Promise you won't go fast," Amanda ordered. Her hands gripped Shannon's waist like a vise.

"I won't go fast," Shannon repeated. "But I don't know why you're still afraid when we ride. Christa is the safest horse on earth."

"Maybe she is," Amanda said, "but then again, maybe there's no such thing as a safe horse."

Shannon patted Christa's neck and shook her head in disappointment. "You hurt Christa's feelings! Now why would you say that?"

"I told you before that I fell off my cousin's horse when I was little! It was a long way down. Then he stepped on my hand and broke my finger!"

"I remember you told me that. But Christa's not a big horse. She's a pony. And even if you did fall off, she would *never* step on you! You've been around her enough to know that!"

Amanda gripped Shannon's waist even tighter. "I know . . . but don't go fast!"

Shannon shrugged. It was useless to pursue the discussion. Amanda would probably always be afraid when they rode. With a tug of the rein and a squeeze of the legs she guided her fuzzy, white pony through the gate and up the hill.

As they rode through rows of pine trees, Shannon breathed deeply, letting the pungent aroma fill her lungs. "I love that smell," she said.

"Me, too!" Amanda pulled a deep breath in through her nostrils. "You're so lucky to live on Christmas Tree Farm."

Just then a rabbit shot across the trail. Christa's head dropped down and she pulled to follow the little creature, but Shannon kept the pony's head up, forcing her to stay on course.

At the top of the hill, they turned left, following the edge of the pines. Silence surrounded them as they moved up and into a ravine filled with tall trees. They could see the shadow of Rattlesnake Hill just ahead.

Amanda leaned forward. "There's Kirkhoff Road." She whispered it, as if someone could hear.

Shannon nodded and urged Christa on, up the hill toward the face. She could see the outcropping of rocks surrounded by tall pines and a few maple trees and bushes. It sure seemed like the perfect place for a cave.

Amanda gripped Shannon's waist tightly. "Look!"

Shannon followed her friend's pointing finger and saw a large buzzard circling just above them. Something in the area must be dead, she thought. Suddenly she had a funny feeling that someone was watching them. She turned quickly, scanning the trees and rocks, but could see nothing but nature: snow, trees, rocks, and the dark blue sky above.

"What's wrong?" Amanda whispered.

"I don't know. I thought someone was here."

"I got the same feeling."

Together, they watched the bushes. Everything seemed still and quiet.

Beside a large boulder, Shannon dismounted and Amanda practically tumbled off with her. "Hey!" she squealed as she landed in the fluffy snow.

"Sorry."

They circled the boulder. Behind it was a big pile of shale and other rocks. Shannon watched as Amanda rubbed her hand along the boulder's crust, searching for an opening. Some parts were covered with snow, but others had been dusted clean by the wind. Amanda's hand stopped suddenly and retraced its movement over a section of the boulder.

"What is it?" Shannon asked.

"I'm not sure. It felt like it was raised up or something." They brushed the snow away from the rock but found that it was just a long ridge.

They were turning to go when Shannon saw a section of rock that was suspiciously wiped clean of snow. It was in a shady area, sheltered from the wind, yet it was clean! She hurried to examine the spot.

Sunlight nearly blinded her, reflecting off the snow and the silvery gray rocks. Then she saw it.

"Look!" she squealed excitedly.

Amanda looked, then gasped.

Shannon removed her gloves and ran her fingers over the indentations in the rock. Carved into it in jagged, uneven stick letters were three short words . . . "Ahrwud and Frieda."

three

The girls stared at the rock in amazement. The letters were not deep. It was as though they had been scratched into the rock with a sharp object. Shannon looked around. Had the carving been done recently? Or long ago? Snow *had* been wiped from the rock. That much was obvious. But there were no tracks in the snow. No sign that anyone had come and gone.

Amanda touched the rock lightly, running her fingers across the letters. "What do you think?" she asked.

"I don't know." Shannon wasn't sure why she was whispering, or why she still had that awful feeling that someone was watching them.

She pulled the gloves on again. "Let's get out of here," she whispered.

Christa's hooves clicked against the rocks where the snow had been blown clear. She picked her way down the hill and through the valley, toward home. Shannon and Amanda didn't talk for awhile. It was quiet in the hills, hauntingly quiet.

Shannon reached down and patted Christa's neck. She loved her pony. Something about having Christa with her made her feel braver.

Even if something back there was watching us, she thought, *I have Christa to keep me safe. No one can run as fast as my pony. Not even a ghost.*

But who carved that in the rock? she wondered. *Ahrwud and Frieda?* She could still see the words, even feel them under her fingertips, though she and Amanda were leaving the rocks and boulders far behind.

"Do you think the ghost of Ahrwud or Frieda carved their names?"

Amanda's voice echoing her own thoughts startled Shannon. She sat up straighter in the saddle and considered the question.

"I don't know," she finally answered, "but it looks too new to have been there a long time."

"Larry did tell the story right outside, in the open, where anyone could hear," Amanda said.

Shannon shivered. "I just don't know," she said again. "Maybe one of the people who searched for the mine earlier carved it."

"Yeah," Amanda agreed. "It could have been someone else."

"Suppose it was Ahrwud, though. Suppose it was his way of asking for help?"

"Larry didn't say anything about the carving in the rock. If it had been there for a long time, he would have told us."

Shannon rubbed Christa's neck. She was thinking of things they could do to find out more. "Let's go to the library," she suggested. "Maybe we can find out something about the legend there."

"That's a great idea!"

Shannon nudged Christa into a trot. "If we hurry, Mom can take us today, on her way into town to get groceries."

"Sssh!" The librarian gave Shannon and Amanda a stern look. They *had* been talking a little too loud, Shannon realized. They were sitting on the floor, leafing through books in the section on legends, looking for something—anything—about the legend of the lost silver mine. So far they hadn't found one single thing.

Amanda leaned close to Shannon and whispered, "I checked the computer. It said all the books on legends are in this section."

Shannon sighed with discouragement. Then she saw a pair of brown leather shoes connected to legs with stockings, and a pink, flowered skirt.

"Can I help you girls with something?" The librarian had lost her stern look. "You seem to be having trouble locating what you want."

Shannon stood up and brushed off her jeans. "Yes," she said. "We want to find something about the legend of the lost silver mine of Silver Run."

"I see," the librarian said. "Well, we don't have anything about local legends in the children's section. But we do have one book in Adult Reference. In fact, it was published by the library itself."

The librarian turned on her heel and hurried across the carpeted floor into the never-ending silence of the adult area. The girls trailed behind.

Just behind the information desk, the librarian reached down and pulled a book from a shelf. She handed it to the girls. "Remember to try and be a little quieter." She smiled before she walked away.

Shannon looked at the cover of the paperback

book in her hands. "Ghosts and Legends of Carroll County, Maryland," she read. "Compiled by Jesse Glass. Published by the Carroll County Library. Let's go to the study section," she whispered.

Amanda followed, through the rows of books and into the empty study section. They shared a chair at a desk in a cubicle. Shannon turned the pages until she saw a chapter titled "The Haunted Silver Mine."

"Read it out loud," Amanda whispered. "No one else is around."

"Everybody knows the town of Silver Run, located on the Gettysburg Pike about nine miles from Westminster," Shannon began.

As she read out loud the girls found that the story was just as Larry had told them. It had happened around 1783 and the Indians were the Susque-hannocks.

"Larry wasn't just teasing us," Amanda said. "The story is a real one."

"Listen to this," Shannon said. "It's what happened when the Indians dragged Ahrwud and Frieda to the cave. 'The dance of death began,'" Shannon read. "'Faster and faster they circled Ahrwud and his daughter, making hideous chants and gyrations until the blood of Ahrwud and Frieda ran cold in their veins.'"

"What's gyrations mean?" Amanda asked.

"I don't know," Shannon said, "but I think it's how someone moves . . . like a dance."

"Oh. Read some more."

Shannon traced her spot with a finger, then continued. "'Suddenly the peaceful sleepers in Silver Run were awakened by two soul-freezing wails. The earth trembled and the winds whistled and howled. Over Rattlesnake Hill a fiery dragon with gaping jaws and terrible fangs was striking out in the sky.'"

She stopped reading.

"That's awful," Amanda said.

Shannon could feel a chill. It began at the base of her spine, crept up her neck and into her scalp. "I don't believe that part," she said.

"Me, either," Amanda said. "Remember what Mrs. Baker told us in class?" she said. "Legends are sometimes based on truth, but usually they get exaggerated. Sometimes they grow bigger and bigger until you don't know what's true and what's not."

Shannon nodded, closed the book, and stood up. "There's nothing about the carving in the rock," she said. "I guess we'll never know who put it there or when."

"Do you think we should keep looking for clues?" Amanda asked.

"Sure. I want to go up there again, tomorrow. Maybe we can find the entrance to the cave."

Amanda giggled. "Get real, Shannon," she said. "If grown-ups have already searched and they didn't find anything, what makes you think *we* can?"

"I don't know," Shannon said slowly, almost sadly. "But we are smaller. Maybe we can fit in between the cracks in the rocks and find places that grown-ups can't."

But even as she said it, she wasn't sure she was brave enough to go exploring in closed spaces. It was already scary enough up in the hills. Especially since she was sure that someone—or something—had been watching.

four

The next day was bitter cold. Shannon and Amanda stood at the bus stop, stamping their feet and rubbing their hands together.

Amanda pushed her soft mittens against her nose. "It's too cold to go up to Rattlesnake Hill after school," she said.

The wind cut through Shannon's jacket and she

hunched up, turning her back to it. "I know," she agreed.

At Charles Carroll Elementary School, students poured into the halls, gathering around lockers and chattering about the weekend snow. A path of slushy, wet, muddy footprints made a trail down the center of the hall, waiting for the janitor, who was mopping his way between the students.

It was the last week of school before winter vacation. In Shannon's fourth-grade class, Mrs. Baker tried to give a spelling lesson. Everyone fidgeted in their chairs, giggling and whispering until Mrs. Baker finally gave up. Sitting on a desk, she asked the children to tell her what they were planning to do with their days off.

Billy raised his hand, then stood up and told the class how he was going to Florida to see his grandparents. "It'll be warm there!" he bragged. "While you guys are freezing your noses off, I'll be swimming!"

"I'm not sure it will be warm enough for swimming," Mrs. Baker said, "even in Florida." Billy sat back down. Then she looked at Amanda. "How about you, Amanda?"

Shannon shot her friend a desperate look. *Please don't tell anyone*, she thought. But Amanda didn't look at Shannon.

"I'll be exploring," she said. Then she glanced at Shannon with a smile.

Shannon pushed her finger to her lips and shook her head. She put her finger down. "Don't tell," she mouthed. Amanda looked confused.

"And what will you be exploring?" Mrs. Baker asked.

"Oh . . ." Amanda stumbled over her words. "Just poking around in the garage. My mom is thinking about having a yard sale in the spring. There's a lot of neat junk out there."

"Well, that sounds like fun," Mrs. Baker said. Then she called on someone else.

Shannon sighed with relief. She bent over her

desk and wrote a note. *Amanda, that was a great answer! Let's keep this our secret. Come spend the night at my house on Friday and we'll make plans. Your friend, Shannon.*

She folded the note into a tiny square and passed it across the room to Amanda.

The rest of the week seemed to drag. It stayed cold and it got dark too soon. The two friends couldn't wait until the weekend. Then they would have two weeks of vacation for exploring!

On Friday night, Amanda came with her pillow, a suitcase, and a sleeping bag. "Mom said I can spend two nights," she announced.

"Neat-o!" Ashley shrieked. "We're going to have a great weekend!"

"We?" Shannon interrupted. "'We' doesn't include you. You aren't hanging around us. We have important things to do, *alone*."

"No fair," Ashley whined. "I wish Sharece could come, too," she mumbled.

"Just remember," Mom said. "This is our busiest weekend for tree sales. You three will have to help out if it's busy."

"We know," Shannon said. "Don't worry about Amanda and me. We'll be too busy to get in anyone's way!"

At dinner, Dad talked about Christmas trees. "You know this is our last weekend for tree sales. Christmas is next Thursday," he reminded them, "and I'm going to need a little help from everyone." He looked at Shannon and Ashley. "Including you two! I'm glad you brought a friend," he added, with a twinkle in his eyes. "We'll put her to work, too!"

"It sounds like fun!" Amanda said. Shannon and Ashley groaned.

Dad drummed his fingers on the table. "Tomorrow morning, I want you to take that pony of yours up to the back pine field. Got a customer who tagged a tree up there last month. He was positive that was the one he wanted me to save for him.

Trouble is . . . I thought he wanted it cut. Now he tells me he wants it dug. Wants a live tree, he says."

"The ground is frozen solid!" Mom said with a frown. "How are you going to get a tree out this late in the season?"

"I already have that figured out, Martha," he said. "Larry took the tractor and tools up there yesterday. We dug around the tree and we were going to pull it out, but now the tractor won't start. Shannon, you're going to have to use that pony to pull it out. Larry will help you. We've got too many customers coming in tomorrow for me to go up there."

Shannon thought about all the times she had pulled cut Christmas trees down the hill with a rope and her pony. This would be a little harder, but it shouldn't take long at all, she figured.

"Okay, Dad," she said. "Amanda and I will meet Larry up there first thing in the morning."

Amanda's arms circled Shannon's waist. Christa carried them through the pines again. This time they were heading to the farthest tree field, the one that was just below Rattlesnake Hill. The sun was shining through the pines, flickering its light in checkered patterns on the ground. It was warmer than usual, and the wind had finally died down. Shannon lifted her face to the sun as they followed the broad trail.

Just ahead, Larry was waiting with his hand and chin resting on a shovel. "What took you two so long?"

"We had to saddle up." Shannon made a face.

"I've loosened the roots. Let's do this and get it over with. It's not going to be easy. The sun is making the snow all slushy. I hope that pony of yours can keep her footing."

"She can," Shannon boasted. "She can do almost anything!"

"We'll see about that." Larry grunted as he tied a rope to the trunk of the pine tree and straightened up. He handed the rope to Shannon. "Wrap that around the saddle horn tight now. When I say go, you make her pull. And don't let her get her legs tangled up in the rope."

Amanda swung her leg carefully over Christa's back and slid to the ground. "I'll just stand back here," she said, walking to the other side of the trail.

Larry got behind the tree, put both hands against the trunk, and pushed. "Go!" he shouted.

Shannon squeezed with her legs and Christa jumped forward. The rope went taut. Shannon continued to squeeze, urging the little horse forward. Christa strained hard, her legs kicking up snow and mud and slush in every direction. The tree began to inch out of the hole. Then suddenly it was up on the trail and moving along smoothly. Shannon pulled back on the reins.

"Whoa," she said. Then she patted the mare and smoothed her mane down gently. "Good job," she told her pony. "Good girl!"

A clump of dirt held the roots together at the base of the tree. Larry moved toward it with a roll of burlap in his hands. Shannon looked at him and laughed. Larry was spattered with mud from his head to his boots!

"What are you laughing at?" Larry demanded.

"You!" Shannon giggled, and soon Amanda joined in. Larry looked down at his blue jacket and work trousers. Then he burst out laughing, too. He looked like a leopard!

Shannon slid from the saddle as Larry pinned the end of the burlap into the root ball and began to wrap it around the roots of the tree. Around and around the cloth went, sealing the roots inside. Shannon helped by pushing a stray root into the burlap pocket.

Larry pulled a tiny penknife from his pocket and handed it to Amanda. "You cut the cloth," he told her. He held the two sides of burlap tight so that she could slice a path down the middle.

"A fine job!" Larry said.

Amanda closed the small, blue penknife carefully and handed it back to Larry.

"Now you tie it off, Shannon," Larry instructed.

Shannon had helped ball trees with her dad before. She knew just what to do. She quickly tied the string around the top of the burlap: two wraps, a knot, and then a bow.

Larry bent a wire basket around the bottom of the root ball to protect it. "Better get this tree on down to your dad," he said. "I'm going to work on the tractor awhile."

Shannon nodded and walked around to the back of the tree.

"Come on, Amanda," she said.

Amanda didn't look up. She was stooped down, examining the mud and dirt that had been pulled up with the tree roots. "Look!" she whispered excitedly. She picked something up from the slushy snow and mud, then rubbed it on her pants leg.

Amanda opened her hand. Shannon looked into the upturned palm and whistled. It was a brooch. A silver brooch.

five

Shannon glanced over to see where Larry was. She couldn't see his head. It was bent under the hood of the old tractor, where he was tinkering with parts, trying to fix it.

She took the brooch from Amanda's hand and examined it. It was dull from the dirt and mud, but it looked and felt like real silver. In the middle of the pin was an oval space, a place that could have once held a gem or precious stone. All around the edge, intricate designs were carved into the metal, and at the very top were three initials, F.A.S.

Shannon almost squealed, then caught herself in time. Whispering instead, so Larry wouldn't hear, she asked, "Do you think the F stands for Frieda?"

As Larry lifted his head from under the tractor and pulled a tiny part out, Amanda scooped the brooch from Shannon's hand and shoved it deep into her pocket. "I don't know," Amanda whispered back.

They stood and walked to Christa's side. "Give me a boost up," Shannon said loudly. She hoped her voice didn't sound strange.

Larry watched them climb aboard the mare. They began down the hill, with Christa pulling the tree slowly behind.

Shannon looked back over her shoulder. Larry wiped his greasy hands on an old rag he had pulled from his pocket, then lifted his hand to wave.

When they were out of earshot, Shannon giggled. "Do you think he knew?" she asked.

"I think he knew we were up to something."

"Do you know what I think?" Shannon asked. Amanda shrugged her shoulders and Shannon continued. "I think Larry's been planting *all* the clues. I think he's the one who scratched the words in the rock, then wiped away his tracks with a branch. After all he is the one who told us the story to begin with. He knew we would fall for it."

"It *is* funny that we never saw letters up there any other time when we were riding. It also seems pretty strange that we found the brooch in the dirt of a tree *he* just dug up!" Amanda was nodding quickly, getting more excited as she talked.

"Remember when we thought someone was watching us? Maybe that was Larry, too!" Shannon said.

"I bet it was!" Amanda exclaimed. "He's playing games with us."

"I'd like to get him back real good!" Shannon felt a smile spread over her face at the thought. "I think we should get even!"

Amanda hugged Shannon's waist hard. "Yeah," she

agreed. "We should think of a trick to play on him!"

As they rode through the trees, Shannon thought about how beautiful everything looked. The sun sparkled on the snow, creating shadows beside each tree. Christa's warm body helped to keep off the chill. Shannon ran her fingers lovingly through the mare's silvery mane. "I don't know how you could ever be scared of her," Shannon said to Amanda. Amanda didn't answer, but she did reach down to pat the furry pony.

As the girls got closer to home, Shannon could see the customers walking between the rows of pine trees, saws in hand. Every now and then one would stop to eye a particular tree, or kneel to saw one down. Excited voices floated up the hill.

A curl of smoke wafted from the wood-stove pipe in Dad's sale shack. Shannon could smell the hot apple cider and hot chocolate Mom kept on hand to warm the customers. Licking her lips, she squeezed her knees and urged Christa to hurry down the hill. She waved so her dad would see them and come for the tree.

That evening Shannon stood in her bedroom, rubbing the brooch between her thumb and forefingers. She laid it in her palm and smoothed a finger over the hole where a jewel had once rested. "I bet it used to be pretty," she said softly. "I wonder where Larry found it?"

"Maybe he bought it at a flea market," Amanda offered. She took the pin from Shannon. "We should wash it off."

Shannon followed her friend into the bathroom and watched while she rinsed it under cold tap water. She wanted to pin the brooch to her shirt. She wanted to touch it and make it hers. But Amanda had found it. The brooch should belong to her. Her eyes focused on the initials on the brooch.

"Earth to Shannon . . . Earth to Shannon! Hey, what are you thinking about? You're in a trance!"

"I was wondering about the initials. You don't think the letter F really does stand for Frieda, do you?"

Amanda's face clouded with thought. "No. I still think it's one of Larry's tricks."

Amanda wore the brooch to dinner. She had rubbed it until it was almost shiny, then pinned it on her green sweater. Shannon looked at it and wished again that she had found it. She watched Amanda touch it with her fingertips, then look down at it in admiration before sliding her chair in for dinner.

They were halfway through the meal before anyone noticed the brooch. Shannon's dad was in the middle of a sentence when her mom interrupted him. "Oh my goodness, Amanda! Where did you get that?"

Amanda's hand fluttered to the pin. "I found it today," she answered quickly.

"You found it!" Mom sounded excited. "Where? Where did you ever find that brooch?"

The look on Mom's face startled Shannon. Her mother's mouth dropped open and her fork clattered to the table. She jumped up and rushed over to examine the brooch.

Shannon was confused. What interest could her

mother possibly have in an old yard-sale brooch Larry had laid there for them to find? Maybe she thought it was real silver, Shannon told herself. Then she cleared her throat. "Amanda found it in the dirt," she explained, "beside the tree we helped Larry dig up today."

"It's Grandma's brooch!" Mom blurted out. She looked closer at the initials. "Frances Anne Schmitt," she said softly. "I never thought I'd find it again."

Amanda removed the pin slowly and handed it to Shannon's mom. "I guess it's yours," she said softly.

Mom took the pin gently. She rubbed a finger over it. "Thank you, Amanda," she said. "I thought this pin was lost forever."

During the rest of the meal, Mom bubbled over with enthusiasm. The conversation turned to talk of the old days when she was growing up on the farm.

"My mom sent me out to help plant seedlings with my pop. I was wearing the brooch that day. I was so proud of that pin! I couldn't believe Grandmother Schmitt had given it to me. Even though the stone was missing, I still loved it."

"You shouldn't have worn it to do chores," Shannon teased.

"I know that now," Mom said. "But I was just a little girl, then. We worked all day in the pine field, planting those seedlings. That night, I realized the brooch was missing. I searched everywhere for it, but I couldn't find it. I never did know what happened to Grandma's brooch . . . until now."

Mom gazed lovingly at the silver piece which she had already pinned on her collar. "Maybe I'll get a new stone set in it. Maybe a ruby. If it weren't for you, Amanda," she added, "it probably wouldn't have ever been found."

"I'll be dad gum!" Dad said. "What were the chances of you finding that old pin again?" He shook his head. "You must have planted it with that seedling."

Ashley giggled. "What were you trying to do, Mom? Grow more pins?"

Shannon and Amanda laughed, then Dad and Mom joined in.

When they were all laughed out, Dad shook his head again. "It's just incredible!"

Yes, Shannon thought. *It is incredible!* Then a shadow of a thought entered her head. If the pin was Mom's, it really had been a lost brooch. That meant Larry didn't put it there for Shannon and Amanda to find! And if Larry didn't do that, then maybe he didn't carve the rock either. And if he didn't carve the rock, then who, or what, did?

six

The next day it snowed, but not enough to cover the roads. In the morning, the customers came in droves. They laughed and kicked up the snow as they walked, obviously caught up in the Christmas spirit. One lady even lay down in the snow as Shannon and Amanda watched. Flapping her arms and legs wildly, she made a snow angel, then stood up to admire it before linking arms with her husband and trudging off to find a tree.

Shannon shook her head and laughed. "She acted just like us," she said.

"Except older," Amanda added.

This set Shannon off into a fit of giggles, picturing the older woman lying in the snow with her grown-up classmates, making a snow angel in the schoolyard.

Each customer was different. Some brought their own saws. Others borrowed saws from the sale shack. Some, mostly the men, were very businesslike. They marched up and down the rows until they found the right tree. Then they had it cut, paid for, and roped to the top of their car in no time flat.

The families with small children, and the young couples, always seemed to know how to make it fun. They wandered down the rows, discussing the good and bad things about each tree. The children rolled snowballs and made tiny snowmen among the pines while their parents debated. To these people, getting a tree never seemed like a chore. And these were the same families who always stopped in the sale shack for a cup of steaming hot chocolate or cider, and stayed to talk about Christmas as they sipped their drinks from Styrofoam cups. When they left with their trees, they always left behind a little Christmas spirit and the shack seemed a bit warmer for it. Shannon always liked helping these families the best.

Dad let her and Christa help pull the trees down the hill. Christa didn't mind the ropes like some horses would. She always stayed calm and waited for her mistress to tell her what to do next. Shannon didn't know if it was the warm Christmas spirit that filled her during these times, or the fact that she loved her pony so much, but somehow it never seemed like work.

After pulling several trees down the hill, Shannon stood next to Christa, leaned into her neck, and kissed the mare. *Why can't Amanda see how harmless Christa is?* Shannon wondered. Out of the corner of her eye she caught Amanda watching her, and she smiled.

By noon, the snow had really set in. It was as if the heavens had opened up, dumping tons of angel-like flakes on Christmas Tree Farm. Road crews began plowing and salting the roads, clearing the white stuff almost as fast as it came down. By then, the customers had stopped coming and Shannon and Amanda were free to do as they pleased.

Just outside the barn, Amanda lifted her face to the sky and stuck out her tongue to catch snowflakes.

Shannon brushed the snow from Christa's back and rubbed her dry with a cloth. Then she threw a big red saddle blanket over the pony's back. "Let's ride without a saddle today," she suggested. "We can pretend we're Susquehannock Indians. We can even find something in the hills to track in the snow!"

"Did the Susquehannocks ride horses?"

"I don't know." Shannon thought a moment. "But since we *are* pretending, it doesn't matter," she said.

Amanda shrugged. "Okay," she replied. "But I think we need a saddle. I'm afraid of falling off."

Shannon rolled her eyes. "Don't be such a scaredy-cat! Christa would NEVER dump us!"

"All right," Amanda gave in, "as long as you don't go fast. It feels funny when we don't have a saddle . . . more slippery."

"We'll just stay at a walk," Shannon promised. She slid from the fence onto Christa's back and then put out a hand to help tug Amanda aboard.

The snow continued to fall as the girls rode among the pine trees. They didn't talk, except in occasional whispers.

"Keep your eye out for something to track," Shannon murmured, and Amanda nodded.

A moment later, a rabbit darted out from under a pine tree. Leaping and bounding, he wove from tree to tree, leaving tracks in the fresh powder.

The moment the rabbit appeared, Christa's head and ears shot up. She snorted and sidestepped as the rabbit darted past, then put her head down and began to pursue the little creature. Shannon let the mare have her head. She had wanted something to track, and it seemed as if Christa knew that, so she just sat on the little horse and allowed her to follow the rabbit.

Amanda giggled and held tight to Shannon. "The way Christa is going after that bunny, she acts more like a dog than a pony."

Shannon laughed, too, as they reached another tree and Christa's big nose rooted the rabbit out from under it. They followed the rabbit up the hill, wandering from tree to tree, until at last it found shelter beneath some rocks that even Christa could not get her nose into. Christa stood with her nostrils glued to the rock for a moment. She pawed at the fresh snow, then finally gave up.

Shannon looked to see how far they had come. She was surprised to find that they were almost at Rattlesnake Hill. Motioning with her hand, she asked Amanda, "Do you want to go up and look around again?"

Amanda stared up the hill, through the gray haze of swirling flakes, until Shannon had to prod her for an answer. "Sure," she finally said. Shannon thought she heard a tremor in her friend's voice.

She nudged Christa with her heels, and they started up the hill. The air grew heavy and still. Only the whisper of swirling flakes could be heard, and the occasional echo of the wind dashing against the dark boulders. They rode until they were alongside the rocks. Then they wove between them until they came to the boulder where they had seen the carving of "Ahrwud and Frieda."

"Do you want to get off and look?" Shannon asked.

"No. Let's just look from here."

This time, Shannon knew there was fear in Amanda's voice, and under her warm snowsuit, she shivered, too. Something about this place was just plain eerie.

The boulders were all covered with snow. Shannon pulled Christa up close to the one that had had the carvings on it.

Reaching down, Amanda began to wipe the snow

away. Finally, she found the carving.

Shannon read it aloud. "Ahrwud and Frieda," it said, in those jagged letters.

Then Amanda brushed more snow away. "Look," she whispered.

Shannon leaned closer to the rock and scraped away more snow until she could see what Amanda had seen. Then she froze.

Under the names, a new word had been scratched in the same crooked way. "HELP!"

seven

T his isn't fun anymore," Shannon whispered.

Amanda was transfixed, staring at the
rock in silence.

"Amanda!" Shannon elbowed her buddy. "Let's
get out of here." She backed Christa out of the rocks
and started down the hill.

Everything was still and quiet. It was as if every

branch waving overhead, every bush that huddled protectively around the rocks, was determined to keep the secret of Rattlesnake Hill. Not even the snow, falling all around them, seeing all, would breathe a sound or give up the secret. And all of it, the trees, the bushes, the snow, and the rocks had begun to seem cold and barren and downright scary.

They had only gone a few hundred feet when Amanda yelled out, "Stop!"

Shannon jerked back on the reins. "What?"

"In the snow! Look! Something blue."

Shannon looked. Then she saw what they had almost stepped on. A blue handle poked out of the snow between the mess of hoofprints and rabbit tracks they had made on their way up the hill. She slid from the horse, reached down, and pulled the blue thing out of the snow. It was a penknife.

After Shannon remounted, she handed the penknife to Amanda, who turned the flat, cylindrical piece over in her hand. She eyed the blue inlay and a grin lit up her face.

"What are you smiling at?"

"Proof!" Amanda said. Then, in answer to Shannon's questioning look, she continued. "This is Larry's penknife. I bet he dropped it here after scratching 'HELP' in the rock!"

"How do you know it's his?"

"Remember when Larry told me to cut the burlap? He handed me his knife and I got a good look at it. It was blue on the sides, just like this one."

"I can't believe he would do this!" Shannon's voice rose with bitterness. "At first it was funny," she admitted. "But he went too far!"

As they plodded down the hill slowly, in the face of falling snow, a large flock of black grackles rose from the gully, screeching and cawing angrily. Shannon jumped as the birds glided overhead.

"Something must be over there!"

"Maybe it's Larry watching us."

"Well, let him watch!" Shannon yelled. She felt the anger begin to boil inside. "We know it's you, Larry!" she hollered, but the hair still rose on her neck as the birds squawked and circled.

She nudged Christa to go faster and faster, until they were trotting down the hill. Shannon was hurt and scared and angry all rolled into one. She wanted to get away from Rattlesnake Hill and never come back again.

"Shannon!" Amanda yelled. "Stop! You're going down the hill too fast!"

Shannon bent her head low over the pony's back and urged her on. Pine trees passed by in a blur. She could feel Amanda's grip tighten on her waist.

"Shannon!" Amanda squealed.

Finally, Shannon pulled back on the reins, but at that very moment a rabbit leaped out from under a tree. Christa sidestepped suddenly, then stumbled. She went down on her knees, skidding through the snow until her hindquarters collapsed, too. Both girls went flying, and tumbled down the hill.

Shannon felt herself rolling, her sides scraping the cold snow, her legs and arms flailing wildly. She came to a stop on her back, staring up into the gray sky that was still releasing a thick haze of flakes. She reached up to brush them away and felt pain flash through her side when she moved. She could see Amanda rising to stand just a few yards farther down the hill, and Christa stumbling to her hooves. Amanda came over to Shannon slowly.

"Are you all right?" Shannon asked.

She noticed Amanda's chin was quivering and tears streaked her face. "I'm fine. How about you?"

"I don't know. My side hurts," Shannon said. She pushed herself up to a sitting position, then tried to stand. A sudden, wincing pain shot through her ankle and she collapsed again. "I can't stand," she said. She felt anger and other emotions swirling inside her. Some she didn't even recognize. She was scared. She knew that. And her ankle hurt—bad.

Christa ambled over to the girls. She shoved her warm nostrils against Shannon, as if to check on her mistress.

All at once, Amanda jumped as a dark blur came toward the girls. She spun around. Someone bundled in a heavy coat and a baseball cap was hurrying toward them.

"Are you girls okay?" he called out.

Shannon let out the breath she was holding. It was only Larry. Awful, sweet, ornery Larry. She had wanted to smack him and yell at him for all the tricks, but just now, she was glad to see him.

"I'm okay," Amanda told him. "But Shannon's hurt. She can't walk."

Larry dropped to his knees in front of Shannon. He rolled up her snow pants to look at the leg she was holding and stared down at the ankle. Already it was swollen and turning purple. He felt for bumps as Shannon held her breath. Then Larry rolled down the pant leg again. An anxious look filled his face.

"Do you hurt anywhere else?" he asked.

"Yes. My ribs hurt, right here." She touched the spot gently, then pulled her hand away.

Larry looked at Amanda. "If it were just the ankle we could let her ride . . ." Larry hesitated. "But her side hurts, too. We can't take a chance on moving her," he said. "You're going to have to go for help, while I stay here and keep her warm."

Even as he spoke, Larry was removing his heavy coat and slipping it under Shannon, wrapping the big sides up and around her. "Take Christa," he added.

Amanda's mouth dropped open. "I . . . I can't!" she stammered. "I don't know how to ride alone. I . . . I'm afraid!"

"You have to," Larry said firmly. "Shannon needs help. All you have to do is give that pony her head. She's as gentle as a lamb and I know she'll head for home. Don't you worry."

Larry stood up and reached for Christa's reins. "I'll give you a leg up."

"But what if she runs? What if I fall off?"

Larry patted Amanda's shoulder. "She won't run unless you squeeze or kick her sides. That's her signal to hurry up. Just let her head for home. If she wanders, take the reins, and guide her back on course. You've seen Shannon do it enough."

Amanda started to protest, then she looked down

at Shannon's face. Her eyes were closed and she was breathing as if she was in pain. "Okay," she said.

Larry boosted Amanda onto Christa's back. Shannon opened her eyes. "You'll be fine," she said. "You can count on Christa. She can do almost anything."

Shannon snuggled deeper into the warm lining of Larry's coat and watched as Christa started down the hill. Amanda took the reins in her hands and sat up tall.

As her two best friends headed down the hill, Shannon shivered. Her ankle was throbbing now, and her side burned. Amanda had to make it home and return with help before it was too dark to see.

eight

Shannon let out her breath slowly as Christa disappeared into the falling flakes. Amanda's back had been straight and rigid, but the reins were in her hands and she was heading in the right direction. Shannon crossed her fingers and mumbled a quick prayer. The sky was the same shade of gray it had been since the snow began, but she knew it must be getting close to suppertime. Her stomach rumbled with hunger.

Shannon watched as Larry walked part way down the hill, watching Amanda for as long as he could. Now, as he walked toward Shannon, the mix of emotions began to swirl inside of her again. This was all his fault! If he hadn't started the whole mess with his silly stories . . . Shannon took a deep breath. As Larry knelt beside her and the thickness of silence and snow settled in, she decided she had to know the truth.

Pushing herself up on one elbow, she stared at Larry. He had pulled his cap down over his eyes to ward off the wind and snow and she couldn't see his face.

"There are no ghosts, are there?" She said it plainly, matter-of-factly.

"What?"

"There are no ghosts!" Shannon felt the mix of emotions rise to the surface and spill over. "There's no mine, no Ahrwud, no Frieda, no silver, no truth!"

Larry turned to stare at Shannon. He seemed

startled by the outburst.

"You wanted us to chase your legend, didn't you? You carved things in the rock just to make us think it was real! You followed us when we came up here. You tried to scare us! Didn't you, Larry?"

Larry rubbed his hands together. Shannon didn't know if he was getting cold or if it was his guilt making him nervous. Either way, she didn't care. She just wanted an answer.

"I don't know if the legend is true. I don't know if the ghosts are real," he answered. "The legend has been around a lot longer than I have and a lot of people, grown-up people, think it *is* true." Larry reached up and rubbed his brow under the bill of his cap. "But you're right," he admitted. "I did carve the things in the rocks. I did follow you. I didn't want to scare you. I swear it. I only wanted to give you an adventure."

"But you did scare us," Shannon accused. "Why did you do that?"

"When I was a kid, growing up on the other side

of Rattlesnake Hill, I searched for the mine, too. I wanted to find the silver so bad that I would dream about Ahrwud and Frieda. I guess some small part of me still believes that a silver mine is up here." He swept his hand up toward the hill. "Some part of me believes there is silver waiting to be found. When you and Amanda decided to go search, I started to hope again. Maybe two girls *could* find what all those grown-ups missed."

"That would have been fine," Shannon said. Her voice had softened. "But then you went and tricked us with all those clues. You heard us talking, too. You knew we thought someone was watching and that we were afraid. Why didn't you tell us it was only you?"

Larry rubbed his hands again, and then his arms. "I wasn't planning to scratch anything into the rock. That first day I was up here poking around and I saw the two of you coming. All at once, I just thought it would be funny to leave a clue. I scratched 'Ahrwud and Frieda' into the rock, brushed away my tracks with a pine branch, and hid. You two were so excited when you saw those names! I remembered being that excited as a kid."

Shannon saw the guilt in Larry's eyes and her anger melted.

"I saw you two heading out again today and decided to do it again. It was easy to get ahead of you. The way you two were chasing after that rabbit, you didn't even see me passing by just two rows of trees over. I guess I got caught up in the fun of it and didn't think about your feelings."

Shannon rubbed Larry's arm. He wasn't such a bad guy.

"I'm sorry," Larry said gently.

Shannon was about to say it was okay, that she understood, when she realized the material under her fingertips was thin. Larry only had a flannel shirt on! No wonder he had been rubbing his hands and arms so much. He was freezing! She had forgotten that Larry had wrapped his coat around her.

"Larry." She touched his arm. "You should get under this coat with me before you freeze!"

"You mean you forgive me?"

"Yes." Shannon pulled the heavy fur-lined suede up and over his arms as he slid in beside her. "But don't go trying to trick us again!" she warned in a half-serious voice. "I might not be so easy on you next time!"

Ducking under the coat they breathed heavily, trying to ward off the cold flakes and fill the tented coat with warm air. It was quiet again, but it wasn't an uncomfortable silence this time.

"How long have they been gone?" she whispered.

Larry checked his watch. "About forty-five minutes. Help should be along anytime now."

Shannon peeked out at the gray, snow-filled sky. It seemed a shade darker. "Do you think they'll make it before night?"

Larry gazed out from under the coat. "I think . . ." He hesitated, then sat upright, peering into the white snow. "I think I can safely say yes to that question," he said, grinning broadly, "because here they come now!"

Shannon followed Larry's gaze, then she saw them, too. Amanda was leading a small group up the hill, and amazingly, she was still riding Christa! Behind her was Shannon's dad and several men in paramedic uniforms.

Larry stood up and waved. "We're up here," he called.

Shannon scooted into a stiff upright position. Pain shot through her side, but she smiled just the same, at Larry and her dad, at the paramedics, and especially at Amanda, who sat astride Christa with the most satisfied smile Shannon had ever seen.

nine

Amanda arrived just after dinner on Christmas. Dad hooked Christa up to the sleigh and Shannon and Amanda met him outside for a moonlit sleigh ride.

Dad helped Shannon into the back of the sleigh, propping her sprained ankle up on the edge. She was lucky that a sprained ankle and a scrape on her side were all she had suffered in her fall on Rattlesnake Hill.

After they had climbed into the back of the sleigh, Shannon and Amanda exchanged two tiny boxes.

"Merry Christmas!" Amanda said. "I hope you like it."

"Open yours first," Shannon insisted.

Amanda unwrapped the box and peered inside. Then she sucked in her breath and lifted a beautiful silver-colored brooch from the tissue. "Is it really for me?"

"Yes! Isn't it neat?" Shannon pointed to an identical pin on her own sweater. "Mom had them made for us, so we could remember our adventure. They're just like Great-Grandmother Schmitt's brooch that you found, except yours has your initials and mine has my initials!"

Amanda hugged Shannon, then pinned the brooch to her blouse. "This is the best gift ever! Open yours!"

Shannon slid the paper from her box and lifted

the lid. Two earrings shaped like golden saddles gleamed beneath the tissue paper.

"That's so you remember that I like to ride with a saddle!" Amanda kidded.

Shannon laughed as she clipped an earring to each ear. "The neat thing is that now you *do* like to ride!" she said. She looked thoughtful. "We'll never forget this winter, will we?" she added.

"Nope! We'll remember it forever!" Amanda agreed.

The moon shone in the sky like a giant silver Christmas ball. A sprinkling of stars surrounded the ball like sparkling Christmas lights. Dad clicked to Christa and the sleigh slid across the freshly powdered road as smooth as a skater on a glassy pond. As the trees glided by and the snowy banks beside the road shone white and looming, Shannon and Amanda huddled close in the back of the sleigh, warm under the big woolen blanket Mom had provided.

"This was the best adventure ever," Shannon whispered.

"Yes," Amanda agreed. "Perfect."

Christa's hooves clicked across the frozen ground and Shannon thought about all that had happened. It's funny, she thought, how things turn out. Amanda had finally overcome her fear of riding alone, even though she had taken a spill from Christa on Rattlesnake Hill. Larry had promised to cut back on the tricks he played. But the lost silver mine of Rattlesnake Hill had still not been found.

Shannon realized that every single thing that happened had happened because of another person, not a ghost. None of it was exceptional, except for the finding of Great-Grandmother Schmitt's old silver brooch. Maybe it was silly to have tried to find the silver mine or to even believe a ghost could exist.

Rubbing the brooch that was pinned to her coat, she realized that Mom's favorite saying was true. Every cloud did have a silver lining. For her, the adventure had been worth the scary parts. She closed her eyes and pictured the rocks on Rattlesnake Hill, wondering if the Hill, like a cloud, still had a silver lining.

Staring up at Rattlesnake Hill, Shannon saw a million stars shining in the sky above.

"It was silly for us to believe in ghosts," she said out loud.

"Yes," Amanda agreed. Then she grabbed Shannon's mittened hand in her own and they both turned to gaze up at the place where they had found adventure.

All at once, a blaze of white lit up the sky. A falling star streaked across the purple heavens, right over Rattlesnake Hill. Without a thought, Shannon closed her eyes and made a wish. She crossed her fingers to cement the wish, then turned to look at Amanda. Amanda had seen the star, too. Her fingers were crossed and her eyes were closed.

"What did you wish for?" Shannon whispered.

"Another chance to find the lost silver mine," Amanda whispered back.

"That's what I wished for, too," Shannon said.

The moon slid out from behind the clouds, lighting up Rattlesnake Hill and casting two ghostly white shadows over the rocks above. Shannon huddled closer to Amanda and grinned. "Ahrwud and Frieda . . ." she whispered, and Amanda nodded.

Check out these other enchanting *Charming Ponies* books!

A Perfect Pony

It's the most exciting day of Niki's life! She's saved up enough money to buy her very own pony, and today is the day of the pony auction. She could take home a magnificent pinto or a proud thoroughbred, but she sets her heart on a beautiful white mare instead. When a little black horse with big sad eyes distracts Niki from the mare of her dreams, will she miss the chance to own the perfect pony?

A Pony Promise

Tiffany Clark has to keep her big brother's family secret, and it's not easy. Luckily she can confide in Windy, the pinto mare at Mr. Paul's horse farm. But when Windy and a mare named Stormy give birth within days of each other, there's a problem. It's going to take a miracle for Stormy's foal to survive, and nothing short of a horse adoption can save the day. Will Windy agree to raise another mare's foal?

HarperFestival
A Division of HarperCollinsPublishers

www.harpercollinschildrens.com